I0542567

FRAGILE REPRIEVE

Wild Justice, Book 2

By Debra Shelton

Published by Sonlight Publishing Ltd.

Copyright © 2018 by Debra Shelton

Cover Design by Sonlight Publishing

This is a work of fiction. All characters, names, dialogue, incidents, and places either are the product of the author's imagination or are used fictitiously. Any resemblance to actual events, locales, or people, living or dead, is entirely coincidental.

ISBN-13: 978-1-7327892-3-4

FRAGILE REPRIEVE

*To all those page-turners out there who believed in me
and helped me find my way. You know who you are.
To my mom, who gave me a deep love for a good story.
My daughter who helped dig up the facts.
My aunt who wore out the pages.*

*Fragile Reprieve
is dedicated to the millions worldwide,
who have lost someone to a devastating disease,
that a cure has not been found for—yet.*

Prologue

He pulled the frayed collar of his cheap topcoat up around his ears to protect himself from more that the cold. A shaggy, dark beard and wire-rimmed glasses completed his disguise. No one that knew him as Lucius Wheeler would recognize him now. Gone was the arrogant swagger, the proud look of a man on the rise.

In the five months he'd been a fugitive, his life had completely changed—and not for the better. Cantrell Firearms had been his way to the top. Marrying the heiress, Chloe Cantrell, would have been the icing on the proverbial cake. She was young, beautiful, and naïve when it came to men—or so he thought. Their engagement hadn't even lasted a week before she informed him it was over.

In one fell swoop, he had lost everything he'd worked so hard for. Cantrell's was gone, burned to the ground by an arsonist—a crime they had blamed him for. And now Chloe was lost to him, too.

Lucius would have missed the picture on the society page had the wind not tried to pull the newspaper from his hands. The flicker of a smile played on his chapped lips as he ran a finger over the face that beamed up at him from the newsprint. Chloe looked radiate, her dark eyes laughing and happy. He could even see the dimple in her cheek, the one that only came out when she really smiled big.

The lawyer she introduced him to the morning after the fire, Tyler Reynolds Esquire, stood next to her in a stylish tuxedo. While one arm had a possessive hold on Chloe, the other rested on the silver knob of a cane. The rod was more than the man's walking stick; he moved with a limp. Lucius recalled hearing something about a gunshot wound that chipped the bone in his thigh and a shootout with outlaws in Colorado.

Lucius frowned at the memory of Chloe traipsing off to the wilds of the Rocky Mountains to find a brother no one knew she had. Oliver Cantrell had stipulated in his will that if his son was found he would be given the opportunity to run Cantrell Firearms. The job Lucius wanted and expected for himself.

With a grunt of frustration, he slumped against the building and rubbed a hand over the hated beard that covered the lower half of his face. *I'm tired of running. Tired of not being able to hold my head up. Tired of always looking over my shoulder, afraid of who might recognize me.*

Lucius looked down at the engagement photo again. "I want my freedom back. I want you back." He hadn't realized until that moment that his feelings for Chloe ran deeper than he thought. If given the chance, could he win her back? He gazed up as a cluster of gray clouds swept across the March sky. "I just need a little more time."

He paid little attention as the wind ripped the newspaper from his hands and sent it twirling down the alley behind him. Resolve set his jaw into a firm line. He pushed away from the building, ducked his head, and joined the crowd moving down the busy New York sidewalk.

CHAPTER 1

Philadelphia May 1900

Chloe Cantrell closed her eyes and ran a hand down the length of ivory satin. It felt luxurious. Her fingers danced over the intricate pattern of the Brussels lace and the tiny pearl buttons that followed silk ribbons down to the narrow, tapered waist. She never imagined she'd be wearing the very gown she had only seen in the one picture of her parent's wedding day.

The scent of lilac waft through the room from the sachets, still nestled in the folds of tissue that spilled from the garment box. It had been her mother's favorite scent. Now Chloe made it her own.

"I remember helping your mama into this dress twenty-seven years ago. Exceptin' that you're a good bit shorter, it fits like it was made for you." Auntie Clare draped a big arm around Chloe's waist and hugged her close.

"Do you think she'd be proud of me?" Chloe asked the black woman's reflection in the cheval mirror.

"Honey child, I know your mama's looking down from heaven right now just a smilin' and your pa's sure to be standin' right alongside her with his chest all puffed out."

She laid her head against Clare's ample bosom and sighed. "I wish they were here to see me get married. I always imagined myself walking down the aisle on Papa's arm."

A single tear broke free of her lashes and ran down her face. Sorrow at the sudden death of Oliver Cantrell, almost a year earlier, had of way of sending her heart reeling at unexpected moments. Nothing prepared her to be a double orphan at twenty-three. Raised by her father for twenty years with the help of Clare and Abel Morrison, Chloe only remembered her mother through the stories the three adults told her all during her growing-up years.

Clare pulled a hankie from her sleeve and dabbed at Chloe's cheeks. "There now, don't go a cryin' and makin' your face all blotchy. Mr. Tyler is expectin' to see a beautiful bride come walking down that aisle come noontime."

Chloe turned and put her hands in the older woman's. "Oh, Auntie, I'm so happy and sad all at the same time. I'm doing the right thing, aren't I?"

The black woman pursed her full lips and raised a dark eyebrow. "Abel and I come to know Mr. Tyler a good bit over the last few months, and I'd say you've picked yourself a mighty fine man in that one. The good Lord brought you two together out there in Colorado 'cause he has a plan for you. Now it's your job to figure out what that plan be. Fallin' in love and gettin' hitched is just the beginnin' of a wonderful life, so don't you start fussin' and worryin'. Today is your weddin' day. Be happy, child, that's all you gotta do."

A quiet knock sounded on the bedroom door. "May I come in?"

Clare hustled over and pulled the door wide. "Come see how beautiful our girl looks."

Chloe turned and looked for approval in the old black man's eyes. "Well?"

Abel Morrison gave an exaggerated wag of his gray head and put his hands on his hips. "My, my, if you aren't the picture of your mother with that raven hair and them dark eyes. Pretty as a picture, you surely are. I'm mighty honored to be walking you down the aisle, missy."

He gave a slight bow, then stood and crooked both elbows. "Ladies, if you're ready I'd be proud to escort you to your carriage."

Arm in arm, the trio descended the wide staircase. Dressed in her own version of finery, Clare fussed with the buttons that trailed down the front of her best Sunday outfit. "I think the bit of extra lace you gave me was just the thing this old suit needed. Dyeing it red did the trick, don't you think, Abel?"

Together they stopped on the bottom step. Abel released the ladies' arms and moved to open the door. "Yes, my dear, you look like a lovely rose in full bloom."

Chloe smiled. She hoped she and Tyler would share the same depth of love when they reached their sixties.

The bell rang just as Abel laid his hand on the knob. The beveled glass pattern cast the shape on the other side into dozens of pieces.

"Who could that be, callin' on this of all days?" Clare huffed.

"Don't you worry none, I'll send whoever it is away. We've got us a wedding to get to." Abel opened the ornate front door to reveal a bespectacled, dark-bearded stranger. His threadbare topcoat and his rundown shoes had seen better days.

"I'm sorry, sir. If you're looking for a handout, now is not a good time. Perhaps you should try the mission down on Fifth Street."

Before Chloe could get a better view of their caller, Abel moved to close the door. A foot stopped its forward motion, and a hand pushed back, causing Abel to stumble.

"I need to speak to Chloe." The man stepped into the foyer and looked up to where Chloe and Clare stood on the last step.

She gasped in shock, realizing who she was looking at. A flurry of emotions surged through her. Hurt and anger fought for position. Anger won out.

"What are you doing here?" Without taking her eyes off the unwanted visitor, Chloe released Clare's arm. "Auntie, call the police. Abel, get me father's gun."

CHAPTER 2

Lucius put his hands up. "Now Chloe, I just came to talk to you." It took everything in him to appear humble and contrite. "Please, give me two minutes. That's all I ask." He hated groveling, but if that's what it would take to get her to listen, he'd do it. He risked a lot coming here. More than his self-esteem was on the line. His very freedom depended on how convincing he could be.

Chloe stepped down to the marble floor. "You have two minutes, Lucius, and that's all."

"Can we go into the parlor where we can talk in private?" He eyed the black couple. The big woman's hand gripped the slim candlestick shaft of the nickel-plated phone. Her fingers poised to pick up the receiver.

"I can get an operator in two shakes."

The old man in the butler suit stepped to a marble-topped table and retrieved a small derringer from the drawer. It wasn't the same gun Abel held on him before, but at close range it was just as deadly.

"You can put that away. I'm not here to cause any harm. I just want to say my peace."

"You're wasting time." The old man made a point of looking at the tall grandfather clock standing next to the door that led to the study.

Chloe made her way into the parlor and took up a position next to the fireplace. She looked stunning. The old-fashion ivory gown was not at all what Lucius would have expected her to wear, but he could tell from the rich fabric and exquisite details, it must have cost handsomely.

He ignored the obvious reason for her attire and focused on why he was there. Lucius pulled off his hat and ran a hand through the hair he had allowed to grow long. He wet his lips and took a deep breath. "First off, I want you to know I'm truly and honestly sorry for any pain I've caused you. I never intended to hurt you. I had a demon inside me. It's gone now. I'm a changed man. No more gambling."

Lucius worked what he hoped was a contrite expression onto his face and searched hers for a reaction. There was none. She wasn't giving an inch. He would have to step it up to convince her. "It's hard to admit, but it took losing everything to realize what's important to me." He came to stand in front of her and reached for her hand.

She pulled it from his grasp and crossed her arms. "Lucius, please…"

"No, wait. Let me finish. It's true, I wanted Cantrell's. I felt like I earned the right to run the business. And, marrying you would have secured that for me, then I realized I wanted you too. I love you, Chloe, and I'm asking you to give me another chance. Don't go through with this wedding. Give me a month to prove myself to you."

Chloe turned away and reached for a small glass figurine on the mantel, careful to avoid the still warm ash smoldering behind the ornate screen. "What about the charges against you? You stole money from a man that loved you like a son."

"When I took that money from your father's company I intended to replace it." He paced. "Things just got out of control. Some really bad men were pressuring me, and I was getting threats. For about two minutes, I even thought about burning the place down to collect the insurance money and get them off my back." He came to a stop behind her. "But I swear to God, it wasn't me that set that fire."

"Then who was it?"

Lucius and Chloe both turned. Tyler Reynolds stood in the archway, his legs spread and his arms folded across the black and white front of his tuxedo.

Tyler hated the fact he didn't have a clue what was going on. Andrew had been giving him a hard time in the backroom at the church when a coachman barged into the room.

"Come quick, Mr. Reynolds, there's trouble at the Cantrell house."

"Andrew, get help and meet me there." He raced after the stranger as best as his bum leg would let him. His stomach twisted. What could be wrong? Was Chloe hurt or sick? Tyler sat on the edge of the seat for the short ride and climbed out before the coach came to a complete stop in front of the big brick house.

Abel must have been watching for him. The front door stood open. "It's Lucius Wheeler. They're in there." Abel pointed to the parlor.

"Thanks for sending the coachman for me. Chloe shouldn't have to deal with that man, especially today."

"I'm just glad the church is only a block and a half away." Abel pulled the small, palm-sized gun out of his jacket pocket. "I had this just in case." He handed the derringer to Tyler.

Clare stood next to the stairs ready to do battle if necessary, a formidable looking rolling pin in her hand. "He's doing a lot of beggin' and sweet-talkin', but I think our girl sees right through him. At least I hope so."

Tyler hesitated in the archway and took in the scene. Their backs turned away, Chloe and Wheeler stood too close together for his liking. He quietly moved into the room and was about to make his presence known when Lucius Wheeler declared his love and asked her to put off the wedding.

His heart lurched when she didn't give the man a negative answer and instead asked a question. Would she consider his request? After all, they had been engaged at one time.

Tyler's ears perked up when the man mentioned the fire and his innocence. Lucius was telling the truth. He wasn't responsible for the inferno that destroyed Cantrell Firearms. Still, he might know who was.

"Answer my question, Wheeler. If it wasn't you that started that fire, then who did?" He eased the hand holding the pistol behind his back out of sight.

Lucius and Chloe both turned. The surprise on their faces confirmed neither of them had seen or heard him come into the room. Chloe stepped past Wheeler and moved to Tyler's side. A mix of relief and confusion crossed her face as she touched his arm and smiled up at him.

"I'm so glad you're here, but how did you know?"

"Abel sent for me."

"He didn't need to do that." Lucius put his hat back on and squared his shoulders. "What I have to say to Chloe is nobody else's business." He shifted his eyes to Chloe. "I meant what I said, Chloe. Think about it. I'll contact you in a few days for your answer."

Tyler couldn't believe the audacity of the man. He was a criminal, wanted for several felonies. Surely Chloe wouldn't consider his proposal—would she?

CHAPTER 3

Tyler's giant friend, Andrew Elliot, burst through the front door, followed by two armed police officers, startling Chloe. In an instant, the room filled with people.

"There he is, officers. Do your duty." Clare shouted and pointed a finger at Lucius.

Lucius backed away, his eyes searching for a way to escape. A pistol appeared out of nowhere. He waved it at the crowd. "Stay back, all of you."

This was some kind of bad dream, turning the happiest day of her life into a nightmare. Chloe remembered what Tyler had said about a cornered animal being twice as dangerous. She stepped away from his side and started toward Lucius. "Please, Lucius, give yourself up. Tell the judge everything you told me. They'll listen."

"Chloe, stay back!" Tyler reached for her.

She looked back at him. "Please, let me try."

She didn't wait for his answer. Instead, she turned toward the man she'd planned to marry at one time. The man she thought her father had picked to be her husband until she found his letter telling her to follow her dreams and her heart. Oliver Cantrell's loving words had released her to chase her own future—a future that included Tyler Reynolds.

"Lucius, I believe you. I know you cared for the company too much to purposely destroy it. And as far as the money goes, I've covered all the debts and wages. We can work this out. Please, you're only making things worse for yourself."

Chloe watched a muscle work under the scraggly beard, and the panic in his eyes turn to defeat. The confident, often arrogant persona was gone, replaced by desperation and fear.

"I don't want to go to jail. I'll kill myself first." Lucius brought the gun up and pressed it to the side of his head.

"Listen, Wheeler, you give yourself up without a fight, and I'll help you get a good attorney." Tyler offered.

"We already know you didn't set the fire at Cantrell's." Andrew stepped up next to Tyler.

Lucius jolted. A look of surprise crossed his face. "You're the guy from Johnny Blue's, the big one at the door!"

Andrew pulled a badge from an inside pocket. "Pinkertons. I was undercover. You give us everything you know on Blue and I'll see if I can make things go easier for you."

Chloe held out her hand. "Please, Lucius. Give me the gun."

No one moved. The room, along with its occupants, seemed to hold a collective breath. A log popped in the fireplace, sounding like a gunshot. Someone fired back. Lucius clutched his shoulder. He dropped the gun and stumbled. "I didn't shoot!"

"I thought he fired off a shot," one of the officers cried, "so I fired back."

Chloe gasped at the realization of what had just happened. The still tableau of seconds ago became a chaotic scene. Lucius fell to his knees and clutched the arm of a chair. She came down beside him and pressed her hand over the one he held against his shoulder. The red blossom spread under their hands. "Lucius, oh dear God. Someone… get help," she cried. She looked up at Tyler. "Please, help him."

❧❧

This wasn't how Tyler expected his wedding day to unfold. He pulled out his father's pocket watch. Both hands pointed straight up. As if to affirm what he already knew, church bells began ringing the hour. He looked up. The tall, white spire in the distance was barely visible through the newly leafed-out trees. "Those bells were supposed to announce our marriage to the world."

Chloe wrapped her hands around his arm and leaned against him as the wagon carrying Lucius pulled away from the curb. "They'll ring again. It's not too late."

He looked down at her. "Do you mean that? You still want to go through with it?"

She gave him a puzzled look. "Of course, why wouldn't I?"

"You didn't tell him no. In fact, you didn't give him an answer at all."

Chloe pushed away from him. "I didn't think I had to. Obviously I wasn't going to consider his request after everything he did."

Tyler watched her face fall as she realized why he asked.

"You thought I'd call off the wedding and give him the month he asked for?" Her chin came up as she placed her hands on her hips. "You must think I'm pretty fickle, or you don't believe I really love you. Well, Mr. Reynolds, we have people waiting for us at that church down the road. Take me there and you'll get your answer."

Tyler's anxiety eased. He motioned for the coachman to open the carriage door. "Then let's get you to the church 'cause I can't wait to hear your answer."

CHAPTER 4

Chloe wiggled against him like an excited child. "Mrs. Tyler Joseph Reynolds. I like the sound of that, don't you?" She smiled up at him, the single dimple in her right cheek announcing her happiness.

Tyler grinned down at her. "More than you know, Mrs. Reynolds."

He wrapped an arm around her shoulders and leaned back against the train seat. They were headed to New York City, then on to Niagara Falls. Philadelphia was as far north as he'd ever been. The idea of seeing the big city excited him, but the prospect of meeting Governor Roosevelt sent a thrill through him he couldn't deny.

The man was a legend. If Tyler hadn't been so obsessed with finding his parent's killers he might have tried to join the Rough Riders when Roosevelt first began recruiting. Now he was going to get the chance to meet one of his heroes, thanks to Chloe.

"Tell me again how you happen to know Governor Roosevelt."

Chloe punched his arm playfully. "I'm beginning to think you're forgetting this is our honeymoon. Remember me, your blushing bride?"

Tyler kissed her forehead. "Never and always, darling. But it's not every day a man gets to shake hands with a great American legend."

"Then it's fortunate for you that father supplied Uncle Teedie and his troops with guns during the Spanish-American War." She quirked an eyebrow at him. "Guess I'm worth keeping around, huh?"

"Uncle Teedie? You don't really call him that, do you?"

"Only in private. It's a family nickname. He'll probably ask you to call him TR."

The star of the evening joined Chloe and Tyler amid a fanfare of clapping and cheers. Although shorter than Tyler by a couple of inches and outweighing him by a good twenty pounds, the man was a giant. He commanded the room with his boisterous voice and energetic storytelling. Tyler couldn't remember what they ate or who the entertainment was, but he'd never forget sharing a table with the man now nominated to take the place of the late Garret Hobart on the Republican ticket for the vice presidency of the United States.

Mr. Roosevelt put down his linen napkin and rested his arms on the table, completely enthralled as Tyler finished up his story about how Butch Cassidy and Sundance Kid got away during the shootout at the Bassett Ranch. The account over, the governor rubbed his hands together and wagged his head with glee. "Bully good tale. Wish I could have been there."

He turned his blue eyes to Chloe and gave her a toothy grin. "And your escapades with the mountain lion make me a bit jealous. I never feel more alive than when I'm out in God's country pitting myself against nature's beasts. My time in the Dakotas, are some of my fondest memories."

Roosevelt pushed back from the table and stood, signaling an end to the evening. He extended a hand to Tyler. "Sir, I believe we're kindred spirits. Could you see your way clear to stop by my office tomorrow, I have something I'd like to propose to you?" Without waiting for an answer, he turned and gave Chloe's hand an affectionate squeeze. "Don't worry, my dear. I'll only keep him for a few minutes. Trust me, they'll be important ones for your future."

Tyler held his breath and waited for Chloe to concede. He was not about to disrupt their honeymoon with business. Still—a private meeting with a presidential nominee? His mind raced with random ideas of what the governor had in mind. Would he offer him a job or ask him to go along on his next bear hunt?

Chloe gave him her sweetest smile. "Actually, that works out perfectly. I need to look for a special gift, and I know how much you men seem to abhor shopping."

Mr. Roosevelt clapped his hands. "Bully good." He slipped his thumbs into his vest pockets and grinned. "Come by around ten tomorrow morning."

❧❧

Unable to sleep, Tyler lay in bed, watching the morning light creep across the hotel floor. He looked over at Chloe. A mess of raven curls covered half her face, hiding her nose and mouth. Dark lashes lay still against her creamy cheeks. *I can't believe what a lucky man I am. Thank you, God.* Coming up on one elbow, he moved the strands back against the pillow and allowed his lips to brush the lightest of kisses across her cheek.

As much as she was his world, Tyler still felt the stirrings of restlessness flicker across his spirit now and again. Was he wrong to want more? He chose law as his career and yet his days riding the open range birthed a need for adventure he couldn't deny. He envied Roosevelt his apparent ability to be happy in both worlds.

❧❧

Chloe paced the floor from window to fireplace and back again. What could be keeping him? Shopping had been hopeless. She couldn't concentrate and gave up after half an hour. Theodore Roosevelt might have been a long-time family friend, but he was also a man of powerful influence. What could he want with Tyler?

She'd never let on she was worried. Settling the debts Lucius had racked up against her father's company had left her virtually penniless. She owned the big house outright, but its upkeep was proving to be more than she bargained for. The fire investigation for Pinkerton's over with Tyler stayed on at Fletcher and Nolan's, scraping by as a junior associate. From all appearances, their rosy future seemed overcast with uncertainty.

Sharing her worries with Auntie Clare had resulted in a sit-down Bible study of all the verses that admonish us to trust in God. If only it were that easy. Now she wished she'd thought to bring her Bible along so she could look some of those verses up again.

Instead, she went back to her pacing. After what seemed an eternity, she heard the key rattle in the lock and the door flew open. Tyler's face revealed nothing. He dropped his hat and cane on a chair.

"Well?" she asked, eager to know if the news really would prove pivotal to their future.

Tyler moved to the window, his back to her. "He offered me a job." He turned; astonishment in his eyes, and a smile stretched across his face. "Can you believe it? I could be working for the next vice president of the United States!"

She came to wrap her arms around his waist and leaned back to smile up at him. "Tell me everything."

CHAPTER 5

The summer had been a whirlwind of campaigning across the country. Tyler was enjoying himself immensely except for the long absences from Chloe. He wished she were here with him, especially today.

Only a few of the nine private cars of Roosevelt's party remained hooked to the Midland train, taking them into the mountains west of Pikes Peak. They stood together on the observation deck as the engine chugged its way through some of the most beautiful country Tyler had ever seen. "It's breathtaking, isn't it?"

TR swept his arm out in a wide arc. "This scenery bankrupts the English language."

"Someday I want to bring Chloe back here and show her the Pikes Peak that Mrs. Bates wrote about in her poem 'America'."

"I believe it is not what we have that will make us a great nation; it is the way in which we use it. I want to save beautiful vistas like this for our grandchildren and great-grandchildren to enjoy."

An hour past their scheduled arrival time, the town of Victor came into view. Gone were the heavily timbered slopes and lush, green valleys they had passed through earlier. Piles of abandoned waste rock pockmarked the surrounding hillsides and ugly steel spires designated the holdings of those with large-scale mining interests.

Victor, City of Mines, flowed across the lower slopes. New brick buildings lined the business district, and a variety of clapboard houses dotted the side streets. The devastation from the fire that had leveled most of the town a year earlier was gone, along with the trees.

As in each of the cities and settlements they'd passed through, a large contingent had gathered at the station. TR waved from the platform and gave them all a big, toothy grin, determined to win them over after calling them crackpots and impractical visionaries in the press's presence. He wanted to sway them away from the Democratic view of unionism and the double monetary standard most townsfolk favored.

Tyler stepped off the train first and surveyed the crowd. Most of Victor's twelve thousand citizens had come out to hear the candidate for vice president. Miners, along with their wives and children, had gathered in their Sunday best. Shopkeepers and businessmen closed their establishments and stood beside the city fathers. It looked like even the town's soiled doves came out to line the boardwalks from the station up the main street.

Some of the children held up paper signs that read 'sixteen to one' and 'Bryan' on them, referring to the Democratic nominee William Jennings Bryan and his promotion of a free silver state. Embarrassed parents grabbed the signs and tore them up.

The children were harmless; it was the adults he needed to pay attention to. Tyler noticed thugs among the citizenry. *I'll need to keep my eyes and ears open.*

A contingent of 'Rough Riders', a drum corps, and band gathered to lead the delegation through the center of town to the Armory. Something didn't feel right to Tyler. He came up beside TR and whispered, "Sir, we're running way behind schedule. I think it would be better if we escorted you and Senator Wolcott straight to the Armory and forget the hoopla."

Although Roosevelt loved hob-knobbing with the crowds of well-wishers, he knew how important it was to stick to their schedule. Or maybe he was also reading the disquiet in the crowd. "Lead the way, my man."

Tyler turned to the town's mayor. "Mr. Franklin, sir, I think it would be wise if we forego the parade and moved right to the hall."

The be-whiskered dignitary doffed his top hat and proceeded to lead them down a side street to the newly built Armory. Inside, the room was already filled to capacity. The majority appeared to be made up of more of the rabble-rousers and thugs Tyler had noticed before. Toughs looking for a fight. He wished now he had talked TR into having a larger contingent of bodyguards with him. A sidearm would have been handy to ensure things didn't get out of hand.

The speeches commenced. Senator Wolcott introduced Governor Roosevelt to less than rousing applauses. Before Roosevelt had said a dozen sentences someone shouted "How about international bimetallism?" and the trouble began.

TR ignored the question and tried to continue. Catcalls and jeers rang out. One or two men stood and demanded them to stop. The toughs were swift to escort them from the building. Tyler could fill the tension rise. He stepped up to TR's side and whispered in his ear. "I believe we're done here. Let's get you back to the station."

Through a low ground fog, the Rough Riders escorted the carriage back to the depot. The mob kept pace and surged around the building. A brute worked his way through the crowd with what was left of a Bryan banner on a pole.

Before Tyler or anyone figured out what he intended, the man gave the stout shaft a violent swing. The end slammed into the leg of a Rough Rider causing the horse beneath him to stagger and sidestep in panic. The pole broke with the impact. Tyler dove to get in front of TR.

Too late. The beam bounced and struck Roosevelt on the shoulder and chest, knocking his pince-nez off and leaving him half-blind and open to attack.

A man stepped out of the crowd. With a mighty bellow, he reared back and planted a powerful right hook into the assailant's face, sending him sprawling back into the men behind him. Several went down. Pandemonium broke out.

"Give him cover!" Tyler shouted as he pushed in front of Roosevelt to offer his own back as a target.

He hurried TR toward the station. The attacker and his cohorts hadn't given up yet and were heading for them. Mob mentality swiftly replaced civility. Hooligans began hurling whatever was at hand. A rock hit Tyler on the forehead. "Son of a gun…"

He looked up from his bloody fingers to see the horsemen create a wall, allowing them to get to the train. Rocks, bottles, and tin cans pelted the steel sides of Roosevelt's private car as they climbed aboard. "Stay down! They're aiming for the windows!"

Tyler risked a peek. The first thing he noticed were two policemen standing against a building, observing the chaos and doing nothing. Sympathizers. "Get this train moving," he shouted.

Out of line with any windows, Roosevelt stood and dusted off his Prince Albert coat and settled his eyeglasses back on his nose. "Before we go, I want the name of the brave man who ran into the fray and knocked that brute to the ground."

As the train built up steam and pulled away from the station, Tyler stepped to the back platform. He spied TR's rescuer standing with hands on his hips, defying anyone to get past him. Tyler cupped his hands around his mouth. "Hey, you there, what's your name?"

The big man turned and grinned up at him. "Daniel Sullivan, Postmaster." The man saluted his farewell.

Unlike their neighbors seven miles south, Cripple Creek welcomed their honored guest. They sat down to a lavish supper at the National Hotel, then moved to the Lyric Theater where Roosevelt gave a rousing speech.

The resilient, indomitable spirit of his employer amazed Tyler. TR acted as if nothing troublesome had happened; only mentioning it at the end when he paid tribute to Mr. Sullivan for his act of courage.

Later that night, Tyler sat with pen in hand.

> *My Darling Wife,*
> *As I travel through the unbelievable*
> *grandeur of the Colorado Rockies, I can't*
> *help but wish you were here beside me,*
> *experiencing the wonders of God's creation.*
> *To say I miss you is a huge understatement.*
> *Today I saw a man stand tall against*
> *strong opposition. He showed me what a*
> *truly great American he is. I only hope he*

will have the opportunity to guide this country someday. We would all be better for it.

It's been an extremely long day, but as I promised I am writing even if it's only a few lines. Your last letter was a comfort to my lonely soul. As always, give Clare and Abel my best.

With undying devotion and love,
Tyler

CHAPTER 6

Chloe folded the letter and added it to the stack. Nine letters in five weeks was exceptional for any man, but they did little to combat her loneliness. She needed something to occupy her time besides getting in Auntie Clare's way or puttering in the garden.

She reached for the newspaper Abel had brought in and laid on the corner of the desk. On the second page was the announcement that an unscheduled hearing would take place this morning in front of the judge, trying the case against Lucius Wheeler.

Frustration bubbled up in Chloe. How could Mr. Stanley not inform her? She was entitled to be included in any proceedings having to do with her father's business and Lucius' trial. Irritated, she when to the hall phone and had the operator put her through to Mattson Stanley's office.

"Mr. Stanley, Chloe Reynolds here." Without wasting time with pleasantries, she dove right into the purpose of her call. "Why do I have to read about a new hearing in the paper?"

Unruffled by her abrupt tone, the attorney replied. "I was just about to call you. It seems a reporter got wind of this before my office was informed. I assure you, I have no intention of keeping you out of the loop."

Pacified, Chloe advised him she would be in the courtroom at one o'clock and said goodbye. Hanging up the phone, she headed to the kitchen where she could hear Clare singing "Shall We Gather at the River" in her beautiful alto voice. Chloe waited until she reached the end and applauded. "You could be a singer at the Academy of Music or Carnegie Hall."

Clare waved a flour-covered hand at her and snorted. "Them high-falutin' people don't care none to hear the likes of some big Negro woman. What you plannin' on doing with yourself this fine day?"

"That's what I came to tell you. I'm going to the courthouse. It seems there's another hearing scheduled that I just found out about."

"They should quit wastin' everyone's time and lock that man away. We all know he be guilty as Satan himself." She went back to kneading dough. "Having potpie for supper so you be back on time."

Chloe kissed her cheek. "Yes, ma'am. Shouldn't be any later than four."

๛

The bailiff brought Lucius out, shackled hand and foot. He looked terrible. His hair had grown even longer and lay unkempt on his shoulders. Gray now streaked his shaggy beard. *He looks old and defeated.* Despite everything, Chloe felt sorry for him. He seemed to have completely lost his identity and sense of worth.

His attorney stood to address the court. "Your Honor, my client is not a violent criminal. We ask the court's permission to remove these manacles during this proceeding."

Judge McPherson's beetled eyebrows gathered as he contemplated the request. "Let the record show that I am allowing the restrains to be removed during this hearing, but Mr. Wheeler, do not give me any cause to regret that decision." He motioned to the bailiff. "Joseph, please stand behind the defendant as a reminder."

Chloe sat and listened to the back and forth legal talk as each attorney stood. None of it made sense to her. Her mind wandered. A sudden burst of motion drew her eyes to the defendant's table. Lucius stood with his arm locked around the bailiff's throat and the man's own gun pointed at his head. His startled attorney stumbled out of his chair in his attempt to get out of the way.

"Nobody move," Lucius shouted. There were only eight people in the courtroom. Everyone froze, including Chloe. *I can reason with him. He listened to me before, he'll do it again.* "Lucius, put the gun down. You're only making matters worse."

"You have no idea what worse is." He spat back at her. "I can't live another day in that hellhole they call a jail." He backed the bailiff to the side door they had entered earlier. "He's going with me until I'm clear of this building. Anybody tries to stop us will get this man killed."

Before Chloe or anyone else could respond, Lucius and his prisoner disappeared. The minute the door swung shut behind them, the judge bellowed. "Call the police! I want that man apprehended immediately." He pointed at the defense attorney, an angry scowl on his face. "No one makes a fool of this court. You and your client can expect to feel the full weight of the law when Mr. Wheeler is brought back before me." He slammed his gavel down, causing Chloe to jump. "Court's adjourned."

The big double doors swung open, allowing a squad of police officers to rush into the room with guns drawn. "They went that way." Mr. Stanley directed them to the other side of the room. He turned to Chloe, his face ashen. "I'm so sorry, my dear. It looks like this nightmare isn't likely to end soon, but Mr. Wheeler just put the final nail in his own coffin." He came over and crooked his arm. "May I escort you home?"

The initial shock of what just happened over, Chloe shook her head. "No thank you, Mr. Stanley. I need to speak to whoever is in charge of catching Lucius. I know him better than anyone else. He's desperate. If they push him, someone could get hurt."

Instead of waiting for the man's reply, Chloe hurried from the courtroom. Once outside, she followed the sound of raised voices around the east side of the building. A group of men stood around a central figure. As Chloe got closer, she could see it was the bailiff, his hand holding a folded cloth to the back of his head. A tall, gruff-looking man was asking questions and shouting out orders. Chloe waited until the majority of the officers hurried away to do his bidding, then stepped forward. "Excuse me, Sergeant."

"It's Captain, ma'am." He looked her up and down. "I'm sorry, but you must excuse me. We have a dangerous fugitive on the loose. I advise you to go home and lock your doors."

Chloe mustered up her courage and put on her most serious face. "That's just it—he's not dangerous. Lucius Wheeler may be desperate, but he wouldn't intentionally hurt anyone."

The captain scoffed and pointed to the bailiff being led away. "What do you call that?" He planted his hands on his hips. "No offense, ma'am but you don't know what you're talking about. Go home and let us do our work. You do-gooders want us to let every criminal in jail free and then holler the loudest when you're their next victim."

Chloe realized she would get nowhere with the man, but had to give it one last try. "He's just afraid of being locked up. Can you blame him? Please," she pleaded, "when you find him, give him the option to surrender."

Instead of answering her, he whistled and waved down a cabriolet. "Take this lady home," he shouted to the driver.

Chloe had no choice. She allowed the cabbie to help her up into the two-wheeled conveyance.

CHAPTER 7

Tyler didn't like leaving Chloe with Lucius still on the loose. He'd been home for a week, but was about to leave on another campaign tour, this one closer to home. "I'll be back in three days. Until then I've asked Andrew to check in on you every day."

Chloe continued putting clean clothes in his valise. "It's been thirteen days. I don't think you have to worry. Lucius is smart. He wouldn't stick around."

Tyler turned her around and pulled her against him. "You're probably right, but I'm not taking any chances."

Chloe ran her hands down the front of his shirt. "We'll be fine, but I wish you didn't have to go again so soon. I can't wait until this election is over and life can go back to normal."

A knock came on the bedroom door. Abel's voice carried through the panels. "Mr. Tyler, your ride to the station is here."

"Coming," he replied over Chloe's head, then wrapped his arms around her. "Promise me you'll stay close to home while I'm gone."

"Promise." She swiped a finger across her heart and lifted it to his lips.

"I'm afraid I'm going to need more assurance than that." He bent to kiss her. The current that passed between them still had the ability to surprise him. "Aw," he growled. "I don't want to go." He laid his head on top of hers and sighed.

Chloe wiggled out of his arms and reached for his valise. Snapping it shut, she handed it to him. "Duty calls, Mr. Special Assistant to the vice president."

He laughed and took the bag. "Not yet, Mrs. Special Assistant to Governor Roosevelt."

"He'll win, you'll see. Uncle Teedie is an unstoppable force even when someone tries to bash him with a stick."

Tyler just smiled. He'd told her about the incident in Colorado, but downplayed the danger. "Good thing my head is so hard." He rubbed a finger over the new scar he now sported along his hairline.

It was the last day of Roosevelt's New Jersey boroughs tour. Tyler scanned the crowd, looking for anything out of the ordinary; a hand hidden inside a coat, a shifty eye, someone trying not to be noticed. The large gathering packed the small meeting hall to standing room only—a perfect opportunity for someone to cause a scene or do bodily harm.

Bodyguard wasn't his primary function as part of TR's staff, but Tyler felt duty bound to provide an extra bit of security after what happened in Victor. He still hadn't talked the Governor into hiring extra protection. TR claimed it kept him from getting close to his constituents.

His training as a Pinkerton agent kicked in when two men slipped into the back and made their way around the perimeter. Both wore everyday workman's attire, blending in with the rest of the blue-collar workers there to hear Roosevelt's speech. Tyler noticed a bulge under the coat the taller of the two wore. Why would someone be wearing a coat in this heat? Is that the outline of a gun?

His heartbeat quickened. He moved to the opposite side of the makeshift stage to get a better view. Tapping the shoulder of a policeman, Tyler leaned in to whisper. "Suspicious man. North wall. Tall. Possible gun under coat."

Without waiting to see if the officer followed, Tyler made his way down from the platform and worked through the crowd, closing the gap. "Excuse me. Pardon me, ma'am." He forced a smile to his lips.

"You're blocking my view, young man. And be careful of my shoes, they're new." The matron stepped sideways, obstructing Tyler's line of sight.

He shouldered around her and looked up. His eyes locked with the suspect's. There was a flicker of desperation, then the man's long, narrow face hardened. He reached across toward his side. Tyler saw the butt of a pistol. "Gun! Get down!"

He launched himself across the five feet that separated them. Stretching to his full length, he slammed into the would-be shooter, sending both of them crashing to the floor. Tyler's forearm came down across the man's throat. The other hand clamped over the culprit's wrist as they struggled for the gun. "Give it up. You're finished." Tyler commanded through clenched teeth.

As if to prove his statement, two police officers grabbed the suspect's arms and pinned them to the ground. Breathing heavily, Tyler stood. The weapon meant to kill Roosevelt in his hands.

"He ruined me," the prisoner shouted and struggled as they pulled him to his feet.

Tyler, the gun trained on the distraught man, followed his glare to the stage. Roosevelt was already being ushered off, surrounded by police. Several men were moving to the steps on the other side of the stage. "Who?"

"Fitzsimmons," the shooter spat the name out. "I lost everything because of him. My home, my job, my family—they're all gone." He looked at Tyler. The struggle over, the man slumped in surrender. "I'm better off dead."

Tyler didn't know how to respond. He lowered the weapon. "Get him out of here."

He relinquished the pistol to one of the officers and moved to an empty chair. Rubbing a hand over his throbbing leg, he let out a long, slow breath. That was close. Too close. Even if TR wasn't the target, the whole scenario could have ended in tragedy.

The evening's event cut short, the hall cleared out, leaving Tyler sitting in the quiet room alone. He needed time to think. He understood the man's desperation and pain because he'd been there. He knew what it felt like—the need to direct your angry at someone—to do something to even the score. *I was just like him until God turned me around.*

Resolved to speak to the hurting man in the morning, Tyler went back to the hotel to check on Mr. Roosevelt.

"There you are." TR saluted him as he entered the spacious suite. "The man of the hour. It appears my decision to bring you on board was providential. Bully good show, my man." He stomped across the room and extended a hand to Tyler. "Can't thank you enough for saving my hide."

"Thank you, sir, but it appears I saved Mr. Fitzsimmons, not you."

"What? The lunatic wasn't after me?" Roosevelt scratched his head and took a seat in one of the high-backed chairs flanking the cold fireplace. "Fitzsimmons, you say. Wasn't he the rotund little banker with the sweaty palms? What'd he do?"

Tyler joined him and sat in the chair opposite. "I don't really know, but the suspect was ranting about how Fitzsimmons ruined him and he lost everything."

TR pushed out his bottom lip and tugged on his mustache in thought. "It's always the little man that gets stomped down when greedy men plot." He looked up at Tyler. "Find out what you can tomorrow. Maybe there's something we can do to make things right."

"I intend to, first thing in the morning."

Tyler entered the police station to a collection of solemn faces. One woman sat crying into a hanky. Another made efforts to console her. Recognizing the officer who helped bring down the gunman from the night before, Tyler moved in his direction. "Officer Timmons, what's going on?" He nodded toward the sobbing woman.

The police officer pulled him out of earshot. "Your guy hung himself in his cell last night. That's his widow." He shook his head. His face expressed his empathy to the woman's plight. "Left her with five kids. Seems Kilpatrick—that's the gunman's name, Thomas Kilpatrick—got behind on his mortgage because an accident at work laid him up for a few weeks. Mr. Fitzsimmons was putting pressure on Kilpatrick to get caught up on his payment, so he went back to work sooner than he should have and caused another accident that damaged some costly machinery. Boss fired him.

"That was over a month ago. Fitzsimmons foreclosed and gave Kilpatrick and his family the boot. They've been living on the streets. Last week, the man's baby son died. Got some kinda virus." The police officer perched on the corner of a desk. "Sad state of affairs, if you ask me."

Tyler's mind whirled. He was too late. He'd planned to share his story and tell the would-be assassin how God got a hold of him and turned his life around. *I should have done it last night. I should have gone to the jail.* Guilt pressed in.

Unable to look the grieving widow in the face, he handed Timmons his card. "Have Mrs. Kilpatrick call me. Mr. Roosevelt wanted me to get to the bottom of the matter and help straighten things out. Now, I'm sure he'll want to assist with the burial expenses." *If he doesn't, I will.*

Tyler left the building heartsick and shaken. The realization that life could turn on a dime hit him full force. He'd experienced it before when his parents were murdered, and again when he was shot, but somehow hearing Kilpatrick's story brought it all home. Maybe because it wasn't just him anymore. Urgency sent him hurrying back to the hotel. *I need to talk to Chloe.*

CHAPTER 8

The late August heat had given way to a hint of Indian summer, so Chloe draped a lightweight jacket over her arm with shaking hands and headed down the stairs. She was delivering an article she'd written and the accompanying photographs to the editor at the Ladies' Home Journal. If Mr. Bok accepted her work, this would be her first published piece outside of the college paper.

Nervous energy vibrated through her as she retrieved the mail scattered on the entry floor where it had dropped from the mail slot in the door. A smile spread across her lips at the sight of the tattered envelope, with a distinctive scrawl inked across its front. "Auntie Clare, Abel," she shouted as she hurried into the kitchen, waving the letter. "News from Matthew and John!"

"Abel, there's a letter from the boys," Clare called through the window over the sink. She tore into the envelope with eager hands. "Haven't had a thing from them boys for over two months. Hope everything is okay." Her eyes and lips moved as she made her way through the single page.

Chloe watched a look of confusion cross the old woman's face as she pulled the torn envelope back up and scrutinized it. A knot of concern formed in Chloe's stomach when Clare dropped on to the closest chair. "What is it? Did something happen?"

Abel stepped in the door, wiping his hands on an old rag. "What's wrong?"

Clare's face transformed. With her eyes squinted shut and a smile stretching from one ear to the other, she did a little jig with her feet. "They're comin' home! Hallelujah, our boys are comin' home!"

Abel grabbed the paper out of her hand and read through the short note, then flipped the envelope over like Clare did. "Well, all be... according to these dates, they should be arriving today!"

Chloe's mission forgotten, the three did an impromptu dance around the large worktable. They collided to a stop when the front door buzzer sounded. Chloe looked at the locket watch pinned to her bodice. "Oh, my, I need to hurry. Mr. Bok said if I'm late he won't bother to look at my work no matter what. He said a good journalist always makes the deadline." She snagged the folder and raced to the front door, Abel and Clare on her heels.

Forty years her senior, Abel still made it to the door before her. "Here, let me get that, Miss Chloe." He straighter his jacket and put on a dignified face before he pulled the door open.

Two travel-weary men stood surrounded by canvas satchels and several leather valises. They raised their heads so that their faces showed from under the brims of their slouch hats. "Dad, we're home!" They stepped into the foyer and embraced their father in a group hug.

"I want me some of that lovin'" Clare pushed her way into the circle.

"Mama," Matthew cried, and gathered her in his strong arms. "You smell so good, like cinnamon and nutmeg and home."

Chloe watched for a moment, her heart singing for the joy on everyone's face, then she patted Matthew's arm. "Can I get some of that too?"

Matt released his mother and grinned down at Chloe. "You bet you can, Squirt." He pulled her close, then released her and stepped back to hold her at arm's length. He whistled. "You've grown into one beautiful woman. Guess we'll have to quit calling you Squirt." He turned to his brother. "What do you think?"

John released his mother and stepped up to rub a chocolate brown thumb and finger on his scruffy, dark chin. "I think you're right. Give me a few days and something will come to me."

Chloe giggled like a little girl. "Oh, you two. It's so good to have you home even if I'll have to put up with your teasing and tomfoolery again."

"What you got there?" Matt reached to snatch the folder out of her hand.

She clutched it to her chest. "Oh, my goodness! I have to go! I'll see you all tonight. Tyler will be back from New Jersey, too. I can't wait for you to meet him." She flew out the door. "Wait," she shouted to the carriage that had just dropped off the two men.

The short ride gave her time to compose herself and look over her writing one more time. It was good—at least she thought so. The subject of the impact of the newly formed National Consumer's League on the working poor was close to Chloe's heart. She'd spent the last week going from factory to factory with the League's general secretary, Florence Kelley.

Florence was an outspoken reformist who followed her father's example, fighting injustice wherever she found it. Chloe remembered her own father telling her how he and Judge Kelley spent many nights huddled over plans to help resettle former slaves after the war.

Florence, seventeen years Chloe's senior, had long been one of her idols. Educated at Cornell, Zurich, and Northwestern, the advocate for women and children ignited a spark of the activist in Chloe.

Mr. Bok read through her story with little expression then sat the pages aside to pick up the stack of photographs. It was all Chloe could do not to jump up and pace the room as he took his time scrutinizing each one. Finally, he leaned his long frame back in his chair and laced his fingers across his lap.

"I knew your father, you know. Good businessman and fair golfer. Shame what happened to Cantrell Firearms. I'll bet he rolled over in his grave with all the bad press and the fire." The editor said with the faintest touch of a Dutch accent.

Chloe bristled. Not only did she want to be recognized for her own intrinsic worth, she hated any implication that she had anything to do with the collapse of her father's company. She raised her chin, folded her hands in her lap, stiffened her back, and prayed a quick prayer. *Help me say the right thing.*

She took a deep breath and let it out, slow and measured. "There's few here in Philly that didn't know my father or his reputation. What happened to Cantrell's at the hands of Lucius Wheeler was unfortunate, but it's also in the past. Although I'll always be proud to be Oliver Cantrell's daughter, I intend to make my mark on my own merits. If my work isn't up to your standards, I apologize for wasting your time." She stood and smoothed her skirt. "I'll just take my photos and manuscript back and be on my way."

Edward Bok came forward and laid his arms across Chloe's work, effectively keeping her from gathering it up. "Hold your horses there. I never said I wasn't interested. Bit of a firebrand, aren't you?" He raised an eyebrow and chuckled. "Draw that chair up here and sit down, we have work to do."

With that, he pulled out a red pencil and marked up a good portion of the first page of Chloe's article. "You're too flowery. You don't need so much description." He continued covering the pages with red. "Let your pictures speak for themselves. They're good, by the way. Especially the ones of the kids in that steel mill. I think I'll use this one for my cover."

He tossed the sepia-tinted photograph across the desk. It was her favorite. She had caught the three children in the photo in an unguarded moment of despair. Their soulful eyes begged for relief from the burden of carrying heavy loads of scrap metal in canvas sacks on their backs. None of them could have been over ten-years-old.

"You've got an hour to clean this up if you want to be included in the next issue." He stood and rolled down his sleeves. "I've got a meeting with my pressmen. Stay here and use my office. When you're done take all this to MacNamara." He pointed out the glass partition to a man hunched over a typewriter.

Before Chloe could reply or even say thank you, the man was striding out the door. "Come see me on Monday and we'll discuss another article."

Chloe fell back in her chair. She couldn't suppress the smile that broke across her face, or the shriek of glee that bubbled up. She covered her mouth and looked out the glass to see if anyone heard her.

CHAPTER 9

Tyler stepped in the door and sat his valise down. "Hello?" He could hear laughter coming from the kitchen—men's laughter—loud and boisterous. Who would Chloe be entertaining in the kitchen, of all places? His mind involuntarily turned to Lucius Wheeler. The man was still on the run. Besides, Chloe would never allow him in the house again, would she?

Hanging up his coat and hat, he made his way down the hall and stood just outside the light that illuminated the kitchen. At the table sat two colored men. Obviously brothers, they had the same large build, a bush of dark hair, broad noses, and full lips. White teeth showed as they both billowed in laughter at something Chloe said. Although they had Clare's size, they were replicas of their father. Abel sat at the head of the table as the proud patriarch, while Clare slid large slabs of chocolate cake in front of each man.

Chloe looked up and saw him standing in the doorway. He didn't think he'd ever seen her look so carefree and happy. *She's beautiful.* Love swelled in his chest.

"Tyler, darling, we didn't hear you come in." She jumped up and ran to wrap her arms around his waist. On tiptoe, she smiled up at him. "Kiss me, please, so I know you're really here."

Tyler obliged and sat her back on her feet. "Aren't you going to introduce me?"

Standing behind the two strangers, Clare laid a hand on each shoulder. "These are our boys, Matthew and John, returned from the Klondike."

"And this is my husband, Tyler Reynolds." Chloe added.

"Gentlemen, please to finally meet you." He nodded in their direction and looked at Clare. "I hope you saved some of that cake for me. Since I didn't ride on the campaign train back with TR, I haven't eaten anything except for a stale sandwich."

"There's a plate in the warmer. You just set yourself down there and I'll get it." Clare hustled around the kitchen, getting Tyler's supper and a glass of milk. "I made sure to hold a piece of cake back for you 'cause I knew these two would devour it in seconds if I didn't."

Matthew stood and grasped Tyler's hand in an iron grip. "Nice to meet the man who finally tamed Squirt."

Squirt? He hadn't heard the nickname before. He raised an eyebrow as Chloe stuck her tongue out at Matthew.

John joined his brother. "I take it TR is Theodore Roosevelt. What's it like working for the governor of New York?"

Tyler settled in at the table. Between mouthfuls of food, he regaled them with stories except for the most recent event—that one was still fresh and painful. They reciprocated by telling him about Chloe as a little girl. The evening proved to be enjoyable, but it had been a long trip, and Tyler still needed to talk to Chloe about what happened. The chiming of the clock was his cue to say goodnight and take Chloe to their room.

Once in bed, she snuggled up against him. "It's so good to have you home. I can't wait until this election is over and we can move to Washington. Of course, McKinley will be reelected. William Jennings Bryan doesn't stand a chance against him, especially with Mr. Roosevelt as a running mate."

"We'll know in a couple of months, but I think you're right."

He let her chatter on about the excitement of submitting her first story and having the Morrison men home after their ten-year absence. He'd had the whole train ride back to work through the jumble of emotions, thoughts, and realizations after the incident and death of Thomas Kilpatrick. Yet he still didn't know exactly what he was going to say. When it seemed she'd ran out of steam, he hugged her close. "I need to tell you what happened in New Jersey."

He relayed the story as best he could, once again minimizing the danger and the possibility he could have been killed. She lay quietly in his arms until he finished.

"How sad and senseless. That poor woman. I can't imagine losing my child, my husband, and my home practically at the same time. How did Uncle Teedie take it?"

"As I expected. He was outraged at the injustice and determined to make things right for the widow. He gave that banker a tongue slashing that left the man cringing and me glad I wasn't on the receiving end."

❧❧

Chloe waited for him to elaborate, but Tyler got quiet. She could tell he wasn't asleep by his restless movements. Something was on his mind—something more than the events of the past few days had him edgy and troubled. It surprised her how easy it was becoming to read his moods. *What's he not telling me?* She waited, anxious herself to share her newfound desires and ambitions, but willing to hold off until he was ready.

It took him several long minutes before he moved Chloe out of his arms and pulled himself up to lean against the headboard. The look on his face set off a small alarm in Chloe's mind. *Something's wrong and he's afraid to tell me.* She twisted around and sat up to face him. "You know you can tell me anything, right?"

He gave her a half smile and wiped a hand across his face, then breathed in and let out a sigh. "I think I need to resign."

Chloe was confused. This wasn't what she expected to hear. "Resign, as in, quit your job? I don't understand. You're the one who said this was your dream job. That you still couldn't believe the soon-to-be vice President of the United States wanted you working for him. What's changed?"

"I've changed. Don't get me wrong, I love working for TR. It's the best job a guy could ask for but…"

"But what?"

Tyler's eyes traveled across the room before coming back to meet hers. "I want to do more." He sat forward to plead his case. "Seeing that woman's grief and knowing her husband had lost all hope because no one would give him a chance, hit me here." He pounded his bare chest. "He needed help—someone in his corner who would listen. Nobody did. The banker didn't. His boss didn't. I didn't.

None of us gave Thomas Kilpatrick something to hold on to.

"I intended to go to the jail in the morning after I got a good night's sleep. I thought it would help if I shared how God pulled me out of the muck and mire I'd made of my life and turned me around." His shoulders slumped. "I was all ready to bombard him with righteous platitudes and Bible verses." He snorted, "as if that was what he wanted or needed to hear.

"Anyway, he tied a sheet around a pipe and hung himself before I even got there. If I hadn't been so worried about getting eight hours of sleep in a warm, soft bed, that man might still be alive. It's my fault he gave up hope. I had a lifeline, and I didn't throw it to him."

Chloe crawled forward and put her hands on either side of his anguished face. "I love you, Tyler Reynolds. You're a good man with a good heart. So tell me what's changed?" She moved one hand to his chest. "Here?"

He covered her hand with his and smiled. "I think I need to do more. There's bound to be thousands of families like the Kilpatricks out there. Hundreds of men like Thomas who are so beaten down they can't see their way out of the hole the system has pushed them into. I'm a lawyer. I know the power the law has and I want to use it to fight injustice. I want to show them God's light in a tangible way"

Chloe laid her head on his chest. She could hear the steady rhyme of his heart. It matched her own. She gave a soft snort of amusement. To imagine she was worried about what Tyler would say when she told him about her new desire. *You certainly have good timing, God.*

"Can I tell you something? You know the article I've been working on was supposed to be about working conditions in the factories, right? Well, it changed, kind of like your heart. At first, all I saw were the bosses and the establishment against the workers, but then I began to see their individual faces. They were all different, and yet they were all etched with the same hopelessness and despair. Here, let me show you."

She crawled from the bed and hurried to pick up a folder from her desk across the room. "These are the extra copies of the photographs I took." She sat down on the edge of the bed and handed him the file.

Without a word, Tyler looked through each one much like Mr. Bok did that morning. He held several in his hand. "These are amazing. You've captured their very essence in their eyes. Those poor kids. They can't be nine or ten-year-old and yet they look ninety. The men and women don't look much better." He shook his head and studied the photo again. "It's not right."

Chloe's heart warmed. He truly understood. "You know I've been involved in the suffrage movement and agreed with my father about slavery, but I want to be a voice for the children. I want to advocate for them like you want to help the poor working class."

"So you're saying you understand me wanting to resign and it's okay? You realize we won't have much money." He waved a hand at the tastefully decorated room. "This house would definitely be out of our budget. A public defender's salary is a mere penance compared to what TR's paying me."

She jumped up and paced the room, her mind racing. "Oh, Tyler, think of the good we could do. You can fight for their legal rights and I can shine a light on their working conditions. Together, we could really, truly make a difference." She stopped and looked at him. "Don't get me wrong, I love this house, but it's just a house. I was willing to move to Washington with you so I guess where doesn't matter. It's the who that counts." She threw herself across the bed and into his arms. "I can live anywhere as long as I'm with you."

CHAPTER 10

Breakfast the next morning proved to be one of unexpected surprises. Chloe and Tyler had talked late into the night about their future. Their first order of business was to share their news with Clare and Abel. As they sat back after finishing the eggs, grits, and flapjacks Clare had piled on their plates, Chloe cleared her throat. "I—we have an announcement to make."

She looked up at Clare, who clapped her hands. "No, I'm not pregnant. This concerns all of us, even you two." She looked at Matt and John. "And since we're all family, we want to know what you think before we make our final decision." She went on the explain everything she and Tyler had discussed the night before.

"Did you pray about it?" Clare asked. "You know it's always best to let God in on the conversation."

Tyler folded his hands over his empty plate. "Yes, we did, and we both feel like God is setting a new course for us. But this affects all of you so tell us what you think."

John and Matt looked at each other. "You want to tell them, or shall I?" John asked.

"I'll do it. I'm the oldest and it was my idea." Matt turned to his mother and gathered her hands in his. "Mama, John and I are done with the Klondike, but gold fever is still rushing through our veins. We aim to head out to

Colorado. They're still making some big strikes there and we want to try our hand at mining underground."

"Yeah, Colorado has to be warmer than the Yukon Territory. I was getting mighty tired of frostbit fingers." John shrugged his shoulders. "Besides, there ain't many women up that way."

Matt gave his brother a hard look, then turned back to his mother. "John and I want you and Pa to come with us. We made enough money to set you up in a nice little house in Colorado Springs, which is just a hop, skip, and a jump from Cripple Creek where we aim to set up a claim." He turned to his father. "Pa, we'd make sure we found you a place with a garden. You could even raise a few chickens if you wanted. What do ya think of that?"

"Colorado Springs is beautiful country, that much I can vouch for." Tyler interjected.

Chloe watched the older couple exchange an unspoken message. Clare got up from the table and made her way around behind Chloe. "Stand up and turn around, child. I gots to be able to look you in the eye."

Chloe obliged, allowing Clare to rest her hands on Chloe's shoulders. "You're a full grown woman now, a married one at that. You've had a good Christian upbringing and I think you've showed pretty good judgment most of the time—like your choice in husbands. Abel and I are right proud of you, but honey child, we're getting old and tired. I'm ready to put my feet up and spend my days reading the Good Book and knittin' baby booties."

She lifted Chloe's chin with her finger and smiled with tears in her eyes. "We may not share the same skin, but you's my girl just the same and always will be. You go with your man and make this old world a better place." She pulled her to her bosom. "Just promise me one thing."

Chloe raised her face to see a tear break loose and trail down Clare's cheek. "Anything."

"Seein' as how my boys here don't seem inclined to give me any grandbabies, promise me you'll bring Abel and I lots of babies to spoil and coo over."

Chloe's throat tightened. Her own eyes welled with tears. It wasn't goodbye yet, but she could already feel the coming separation. I don't know if I can do this. What if I'm not ready?

Tyler must have sensed her anguish. He stood. "Chloe."

Clare dropped her arms, and Tyler gently turned her around and pulled her in against him. "I'll see that all our children know their Grandma and Grandpa Morrison."

"They have a couple of uncles here too, you know. Don't forget about us." John added.

Chloe dashed the tears from her eyes and laughed. "Never."

Tyler sat across from TR in his impressive New York office. Although the man was running on the Republican ticket for vice president, he had yet to give up the governorship of New York State and his desk testified to that fact. This had not been a conversation he'd been looking forward to, but he managed to lie out his future plans in a logical and concise order. TR sat in silence, the scowl on his face his only outward reaction to the news that Tyler was leaving.

"Sir, I want you to know I will always remember my time here with fondness. It's truly been an honor to work under you even if only for these past few months."

Roosevelt leaned forward, his arms resting on the desktop, his hands folded. "Lad, you're being very short-sighted. I think you need to give this more thought and I'm not willing to accept your resignation at this time."

Tyler started to protest, but TR held up a finger. "Let me finish. You've brought up something that has been on my mind all week. The New Jersey incident was unfortunate, but I don't intend to let that man's death be for not. When we win the election, this administration will have an opportunity to address the serious issues concerning child labor laws, workplace environment, the overreach of banking policy, and affordable housing. I started reforms here in New York but we have a whole country that needs an overhaul.

"They call this the Progressive Era, well by jiminy, I intend to make progress. We have five weeks until the election. Stick with me and help me work up a plan of action so we can hit the ground running as soon as the inauguration is over and I'm officially in office. I need you. I need your legal mind and your bulldog tenacity.

"As for that wife of yours, she's a firecracker and a darn good little photographer if this picture is any indication." He nodded at the photo under his hands. "If you want, I can put a word into Adolph over at the Times or Wilkins at the Washington Post."

Tyler tried to suppress a snort. "If I know Chloe she'd have a fit if she found out she didn't get a job on her on merit."

TR laughed. "True. Can't blame her, I'd feel the same way." Roosevelt stood and came around the desk.

Tyler joined him and extended his hand. "I'll give your proposal considerable thought, but this will have to be a joint decision between Chloe and myself."

"Understandable. I commend you for wanting to follow your conscious. Would that every citizen considered it their civic duty to lift up their fellow man."

Tyler had the long train ride home to contemplate TR's request. The man had a good point. Maybe he was being shortsighted. Couldn't he do more good in Washington or even New York than out on his own? In the relative quiet of the near-empty train car, he bowed his head and asked God for guidance.

CHAPTER 11

It had been a flurry of continuous activity for the past three weeks. Abel, Clare, and Chloe stood in a sea of boxes and crates that crowded the library. The only pieces of furniture left in the room were Mr. Cantrell's desk and his favorite chair. Abel ran a hand over the soft leather back. "I'm glad you're keeping his chair. Mr. Tyler will look right good, sitting in it after a hard day helping folks."

Abel watched Chloe fold down the flip on the last box and run a hand over it. "I never realized how many books Papa had." There was a catch in her voice. "I know I can't keep all of them, but it's hard to let them any of them go."

Clare put her arm around her and drew her close. "Don't do nobody no good if they just be collectin' dust. Best give them to people who'll cherish them the way he did."

"I know. I'm having some sent to Mr. Bassett in Colorado. He'll love them." She turned to Abel. "Did you get the ones you wanted?"

"I'll treasure them. Thank you, Miss Chloe." He turned at the sound of the buzzer. "That'll be the movers."

After a late breakfast, Abel held the door as the last piece of furniture was carried out and loaded on a freight wagon. It was time. He went in search of his wife. Clare stood in the kitchen looking out the window above the sink.

He came up behind her and encircled her ample waist with both arms. "Are you ready?"

"You know how many seasons I've seen change through this window?"

Abel stepped to her side and leaned his head in to touch hers. "Many a year, my dear, many a year."

"The Lord's been good to us, hasn't he, Abel? Who would've thought the two of us would be traipsin' off to Colorado at our age? We're just like Israel's children. Born in slavery, but now we be free to move to the promise land. I hope Miss Chloe and Mr. Tyler know what they be doin'. I'm gonna miss her so much."

Abel pulled her away from the view and moved her toward the door. "Now, Clare honey, don't you let them hear you questioning their decision or ours. You know it's time. You're tired and I'm plumb tuckered out. Having our boys close at hand will be a real blessing. Besides, Chloe's a grown woman, you said so yourself. She'll be fine. Mr. Tyler will see to that, and between the money Mr. Cantrell left us and the boys fixing to buy us a house, we're going to be just fine too."

Arm in arm, they moved down the front hall to stop before the double doors to Mr. Cantrell's study. Chloe and Tyler stood embraced in front of the cold fireplace. Abel cleared his throat. "We're ready, Mr. Tyler, sir."

Chloe wiped her eyes and dabbed at her nose. Leaving the only home she'd ever known was harder than she thought.

Tyler kissed her forehead. "All the memories are going with you, you know. It's just an empty house now, ready for someone else to make memories here."

She laid her head against his chest. The steady beat of his heart reassured her she was where she belonged, in the arms of the man she loved. "Promise me we'll create lots of new, happy memories, okay?"

"You have my word." He grabbed her hand and guided her out of the room. "Now, we'd better hurry if we're going to catch our train."

The ride to New York gave Chloe time to collect herself after the teary farewell at the train station. Abel and Clare's train left first. She clung to Clare as long as she could, then gave Abel a hug and kissed his cheek. "Please take care of her and of yourself. We promise to visit soon."

The promise remembered, Chloe turned to Tyler. "We will visit Colorado next year, right?"

Tyler wrapped his big hand around hers and brought it to his lips. "No matter what happens with the election, TR's planning a trip out west, so yes, we will be there come January."

Chloe relaxed. "You think McKinley will win? Bryan is strong in the south and parts of the west. What happens if he pulls it off?"

"Then TR stays governor of New York, I set up my law practice there and you, my dear, become a famous journalist and photographer."

❧

Six weeks after the Republicans won the elections with fifty-one percent of the vote, Tyler sat reading the headlines to the new vice president and then laid down the paper. "I know I've already congratulated you on the win, but sir, I want you to know how much I believe your move to Washington will be a positive influence on this country."

TR got up and came around the table to shake Tyler's hand. "Thank you, my friend, and you should know how much I appreciate you hooking your wagon to mine, at least for the next year. We've got our work cut out for us, what with getting the last of my reforms on the books here in New York before I officially step down."

"Now that we don't have to concentrate on campaigning, we can push some of that legislation through. Chloe's excited about the revised child labor laws and beefing up compulsory school attendance."

Together, the two men walked down the hall of the governor's mansion. "Realistically, changing the law isn't going to do much on the streets unless there's a way to enforce it. More inspectors are needed and a stronger social welfare system with some muscle. Hopefully, Odell will carry forward what we put in place."

"Well, we only have what's left of your governorship to get it accomplished."

The two parted ways at the door to the governor's office. Tyler hurried from the building, eager to get back to Chloe at their rented brownstone. He arrived to a quiet, empty house. A short note rested on a small sideboard.

Gone to garment district. Back this evening. Love, Chloe.

Tyler tossed the note back down. "Confound it! She knows I don't want her going to those kinds of places alone." He crushed his hat back down on his head and charged out the door, rattling the glass as he slammed it shut.

CHAPTER 12

Chloe stuck close to the building to avoid the jostling crowd. Washington Place bustled with people coming and going from the tall tenements that housed a multitude of illegal factories and squalid dwellings. The narrow streets were clogged with drays, pushcarts, and every manner of conveyance.

Even though it was only three days before Christmas, there was little sign of it here. No gay swags of evergreen draped the lampposts. No store windows displaying porcelain-faced dolls or red wagons. The soot-stained snow and gray sky seemed fitting for the dismal scene.

Finding a narrow alcove between buildings where she wouldn't get knocked down, Chloe studied the faces of the passersby. Most were grim and anxious. A few looked determined to overcome their circumstances. The sound of a child's laughter caused her to pull her camera out of her satchel and watch for a break in the crowd.

Across the street, three little girls and a small boy shared the contents of a lunch bucket. She focused and snapped their picture. They should be in school. She waited a few minutes while they finished their meager meal. Done, they scurried down the alley and vanished behind a stout metal door it took all four to open.

Curious, she crossed the street and made her way down the trash-strewn, smelly passage to the imposing steel entrance. White stenciled letters warned her unauthorized entry would result in fines and imprisonment. Chloe noticed a stick wedged at the bottom, kept the door from closing. She pulled on the handle. It scraped open on rusty hinges. She cringed at the sound. So much for making a silent entrance.

She followed the constant hum and grind of machinery up a flight of stairs, and stopped in the darkened stairwell to peek around the corner. Before her, a sizable room stretched to the barred windows on the other side. Sewing machines were lined up in two rows while the back wall held tall racks with bolts of fabric draped from them.

Children—some not much taller than the tables they sat at—were sewing on buttons or making artificial flowers. Their eyes dull and their shoulders stooped, they concentrated on the repetitious task before them. Toddlers fingered scraps and sucked thumbs on the dusty floors. A few babies lie nestled in baskets at their mother's feet while nimble fingers fed fabric under the needles of their machines. Two teenage boys operated the bigger contraptions, and a couple of older men cut around pattern pieces at a long table.

The noise and cold permeated the closed-up room. Chloe, dressed in a wool coat with matching hat and gloves, could still feel the chill of the December air. She shivered at the sight of the scantily dressed children bent to the task in front of them.

With shaking fingers, she focused her camera and snapped several pictures. She had just finished one roll of film and was loading another into her camera when a hand clamped down on her shoulder and spun her around.

"Who are you and what do you think you're doing, lady?"

"I'm… I'm an inspector." She stretched to her full five feet and thrust her chin up with authority. "I'm making a surprise inspection of random tenement factories to be sure they're abiding by the law prohibiting children under certain ages to be operating machinery."

Chloe didn't know where the bravado or words came from, but she reinforced her claim by putting her camera away and pulling out a small notebook and pencil. "I need the name of the company and the person responsible for these—employees."

She posed the pencil over the paper and held her breath. Would he fall for her ploy? He was a big man, twice her size, and had a mean, ugly look about him. *He wouldn't think anything of backhanding me or any of these poor people if he thought he could get away with it.*

She cocked her head and tapped her foot. Nervous sweat collected under her arms. "Well, if you don't know then perhaps I can come back another time and talk to someone who does."

The brute growled and clamped a meaty hand on her arm. "You ain't going nowhere but downstairs."

Chloe locked eyes with a woman at the closest sewing machine. There was fear in their depths—fear and hopelessness. Was she afraid for herself or Chloe? The man jerked her around and marched her back down the rickety stairs. *Please, God, give me protection!*

They burst into a room that was the direct opposite of the floor above. This one was laid out like a productive office. One woman stood at a filing cabinet behind a burly man seated at a desk smoking a cigar. He had a swarthy complexion with thick, dark hair that needed cut. When the door slammed behind them, Cigar Man looked up. His eyes sent a chill down Chloe's spine. They were as dark as his hair and hard as granite.

"Who's she?" he asked around the smelly cheroot.

"Found her snooping upstairs." He pulled the satchel from her shoulder and tossed in on the desk. "She was taking pictures. Says she's an inspector."

Cigar Man leaned back and laced his fingers behind his head. "That so? What's your name?"

Chloe tried to work her voice up around the lump in her throat. "Jane Smith."

"Show me your credentials."

She began to shake.

❧❧

Tyler had been walking for blocks. Every few feet, he stopped people to describe Chloe and to ask if they'd seen her. His leg ached, and his heart drummed with a sense of urgency that propelled him to move faster. *Where are you?*

He stopped and looked up at the grimy brick facades of the tenements that lined the streets and created a dismal urban canyon. The gloom and despair matched the expressions on the faces of the children he passed huddled in alleyways or hawking papers on the corners for three cents. Their desperation was visible to any that took the time to notice. Chloe would notice.

He stopped to lean against the corner of a building and rubbed his arms against the cold. A childish giggle made him glance over his shoulder. In the dim recess of the alley sat a little boy, about seven. Another, a scrap of bright white, lacey linen on his head, clowned and cavorted to his audience. Something about the scene struck Tyler as odd—

out of place. He was about to turn away when something clicked. The hanky! He dashed down the alley and grabbed the square of cloth off the bigger boy's head.

"Hey, mister, give that back."

Tyler growled at him. "Where d'you get this?"

The boy stepped back, guarding the younger one. "Found it right over there." He gave a jerk of his chin. "We didn't steal it, if that's what you're thinkin'. Tommy and me, we ain't thieves."

Tyler rubbed a finger over the familiar embroidery—swirling CC initials. Clare had sewn them on all of Chloe's handkerchiefs. "Did you see who dropped this?"

The street urchins shook their heads. "It was just layin' there, all pretty like." The smaller one offered.

Tyler dug in his pocket, flipped them a silver dollar, and turned to leave.

"Gee, thanks, mister!"

A block down, he spied a policeman standing on the corner, twirling his baton and whistling. Tyler rushed up. "Officer! I need your help."

The man swung around. He was more boy than a grown man, with freckles across his nose and a uniform that was too big for his lanky frame. He smiled and stuck his nightstick in his belt. "What can I do for you, sir?"

"My wife is missing. I need help finding her."

The boy cop pushed his cap back on his head, revealing a mop of carrot red hair. He looked Tyler up and down. "I think you might be better off looking uptown. She's probably been out shopping or having tea in some swanky restaurant. Fancy ladies don't come down to the district unless they're looking for something a little different, if you know what I mean." He jerked his eyebrows up and down a couple of times and grinned.

Tyler's temper flared. He wanted to grab the front of the kid's uniform and show him just how serious he was, but that would only waste precious time. Instead, he balled his fingers into fists and clinched his jaw. He stepped in closer, towering over the rookie. He read the shiny new nametag. "Where's the nearest station house, Officer Peters?"

The kid swallowed, his prominent Adam's apple bobbing up and down, his eyes rounded. "Two blocks south; West Thirty-fifth and Ninth."

Tyler turned away.

"Hey, mister, what does she look like?"

"Tiny. Black hair and eyes. Beautiful. She'll be carrying a leather satchel. Her name's Chloe Reynolds." Tyler called over his shoulder as he headed across the busy street.

CHAPTER 13

"Look, Captain Boyle, my wife is a journalist and photographer, not some wanton woman looking for a fun afternoon on the other side of the tracks. She's working on an exposé of the garment industry's use of child labor."

"Exposé? What's that mean?"

Tyler was losing patience. "It doesn't matter. What matters is that she's out there, alone and possibly in danger. I need your men to help me scour the district. They know this place, I don't."

The Captain stood and hiked up his waistband where his holster dragged it down. "Okay, Mr. Reynolds, I understand your concern, but you really need to let us handle this—if there's something here to handle, that it. Just because you found her hankie doesn't mean she's still in the area. I'll bet your wife's probably waiting supper for you right now. Why don't you go on home. If she doesn't show up, come back in the morning."

The man's nonchalance was sending Tyler over the edge. He wanted to grab him by his lapels and throttle him. Instead, he muscled his temper back under control. "May I use your phone? I need to call the governor."

Boyle came to attention. "The governor! You know him?"

"I work for Mr. Roosevelt. TR is a good friend of my wife's."

The officer stammered, "Why didn't you say so." He stuck two fingers between his lips and whistled. The large busy room fell silent. "Listen up. This gentleman's wife is missing down in the district." He turned to Tyler. "Can you give us a description?"

Tyler filled them in. Within minutes, ten policemen were moving from tenement to tenement, banging on doors. No one seemed to have noticed a beautiful young woman with a camera.

Darkness soon closed in, along with a bone-chilling cold. The only people on the streets were the homeless, and vagrants huddle around small fires in vacant lots to keep warm. Driven by desperation, Tyler pulled the collar of his topcoat up and trudged down the next block. His feet dragged. His leg screamed in protest at the extended exertion and forced him to lean heavily on his cane for support. Anxiety and fear knotted his shoulders, igniting a raging headache at the base of his skull. *I'm not going to give up.* He trudged on.

"Excuse me, sir." The young, freckle-faced cop from earlier slid to a stop beside him. "You're wanted back at headquarters. Captain Boyle sent me to get you."

Tyler grabbed the young man's coat sleeve. "Did they find her?"

Peters shrugged and pulled away. "I don't know. I'm just supposed to bring you back."

"Then what are you waiting for, lead the way." Hope quickened his steps.

The heat inside the precinct felt like a warm blanket. Tyler hadn't realized how cold he'd gotten. *How cold is Chloe right now?*

Boyle came toward him. "Mr. Reynolds, I've called my men off for the night."

"What!" Tyler protested.

The man put up a hand. "Let me finish. We've covered all the buildings we have access to, there are others that are locked up by the owners. First thing tomorrow morning, I'll personally be calling every one of them to open up those buildings. I need you to go home and use your influence to get a warrant to enter any property we can't reach the owners on, just in case."

As much as he hated the idea of leaving, Tyler conceded. An officer hailed a cab for him. Bone-weary, he climbed inside and laid his head back against the upholstered seat. How could she have just disappeared? Chloe, where are you? He slammed a fist into the seat beside him. "If somebody hurt her, I'll kill him."

When the cabriolet pulled to the curb, his one glimmer of hope was dashed. The furnished brownstone they were renting on the Eastside stood dark. Tyler descended from the cab and used his key to let himself in. It felt cold, impersonal, and empty. His back pressed against the door, he stood in the quiet gloom. His shoulders slumped. He released the tight rein he'd keep on his emotions. A long sob shuddered through his body as he allowed himself to slide to the floor. *Help me, God.*

CHAPTER 14

Before the sun broke from the horizon, Tyler was moving out the front door. He started in surprise to find TR situation under a fur lap rug when he climbed into the waiting brougham. "What are you doing here?"

Roosevelt snorted. "You don't think I was going to sit idly by while your wife is missing, do you? When you called last night, I reached out to a judge or two. Blanket warrants are being delivered to the fourteenth precinct. Superintendent Devery assures me finding Chloe will be his top priority."

"I guess being the vice-president-elect and governor carries some clout."

TR snorted again. "Don't forget I was the police superintendent myself before I became governor. I've known Big Bill for years. He'll get the job done."

Tyler leaned over his knees and bowed his head. "It better be quick. I don't think I can handle another night like last night." He looked up at Mr. Roosevelt. "We've got to find her."

The ropes holding her eased a fraction as Chloe sat up straighter in the chair. She was cold, hungry, and scared. Cigar Man and the big lout who manhandled her were gone. The room now devoid of any incriminating evidence that anything illegal had gone on there. Through the long night, she'd heard noises overhead. The sounds of heavy furniture being dragged across the floor lasted for hours, then everything went silent.

She wrestled against her bindings and gagged on the filthy rag tied across her mouth. What if she threw up? She could choke to death on her own vomit. The thought made the bile rise even more. *I have to stay calm. Dear Lord, send help, please!*

Hours dragged. Chloe watched the light from the lone window shift across the floor. Something glinted. It looked like a piece of glass or mirror, maybe. *If I can get to it, I could cut my bonds!*

With a surge of renewed hope, Chloe rocked the chair back and forth until it tipped over with a thud. The stirred up dust made her sneeze and caused her eyes and nose to run. The ropes bit into the shoulder now resting on the floor. Her legs tied down, she could only use the hard edge of her bottom shoe to scoot herself across the worn floorboards an inch at a time.

After an agonizingly long time, she was close enough to see the shard of glass. It wasn't much—not even two inches long with a rounded edge. Chloe recognized the piece of camera lens. When the boss man dumped her satchel, her camera fell out and crashed to the floor, breaking apart into several pieces. At the time, Chloe was heartsick at the wanton destruction. The camera had been a wedding present from Tyler. Now she was elated to know it might just save her.

She worked herself around and felt for the large splinter of glass. There—got it! Newfound optimism gave her strength to work the sharp edge against the rope binding her hands. In the cold of the vacant room, sweat popped out and dripped from her forehead. Her grip on the glass slipped as her own blood began the coat its smooth surface. The shard fell from her fingers. *No! Not now, I'm so close!*

She screamed in frustration. The sound, muffled by the gag, didn't carry past the closed door. Chloe rested her head against the floor and cried.

CHAPTER 15

A young newsie with a small pile of the New York Times under his arm gave them their first break. "I live down in the basement there." He pointed a grubby, newsprint-stained hand down a dirty, trashed-strewn ally. "Last night men were moving lots of stuff out of the building across the way. They seemed in an awful hurry. One of them, a big guy, asked another man smoking a cigar, what he wanted to do about the woman." The boy shrugged his shoulders. "I didn't hear what he said 'cause they were moving away, but I never seen no lady come out."

Tyler slammed past the cop who was questioning the kid. "Come on, she must still be inside!" He raced to a big steel door and jerked the handle. It didn't budge. "We need some kind of pry bar."

He paced back and forth, waiting while one officer ran for something to lever the door open. A rush of adrenalin made his hands shake and spiked his blood pressure. He was close, he could feel it. What was keeping them?

After what seemed like hours, a contingent of firemen arrived bearing various tools. "Stand back, sir. We'll get this opened in a jiffy."

Tyler stepped out of the way, ready to move the minute the door opened. Mr. Roosevelt and the police superintendent, along with a crowd of other officers, flowed into the alleyway.

"Is she here?" the vice-president-elect asked.

Tyler came toward them. "We haven't gotten inside yet."

Big Bill Devery, the police superintendent, shouted at the men working on the door. "Hurry it up there. Mrs. Reynolds may be in dire need of our assistance." He turned to Tyler. "I have one of those new-fangled ambulances standing by on the street. If your wife's in there, we'll see that she's taken care of."

With a loud bang, the door sprang open. Men rushed in, Tyler on their heels. "Chloe!" he shouted. The tramp of feet on the stairs drowned out any response he might have hoped to get. Two men came out of the first floor room off the stairwell, shaking their heads.

Tyler headed to another door. It was locked. With a mighty shove, he slammed into it with his shoulder. The wood frame splintered, but didn't give way. "Give me that bar," he demanded of the firemen standing at the alley entrance.

"No need. Let me in there. I haven't got to bust a door down in a really long time." Devery said. He took a powerful swing with his foot. The wood slab groaned and yielded, crashing to the bare floor. Devery stepped inside, blocking Tyler's view.

"Is she there? Let me in." He pushed past and scanned the room. In the far corner, almost out of sight around a beat-up desk, Tyler could see a pair of feet and chair legs. "Chloe!" He ran to her side. She wasn't moving—her eyes closed. "Oh, God, get a doctor!"

Pulling a penknife from his pocket, he cut the ropes away from her wrists and pulled the gag from her mouth.

Her eyes opened. She ran her tongue over her lips. "You came." She whispered, her voice raspy.

"I need some water over here." Tyler shouted, gathering Chloe in his arms as he sat on the floor. "Thank God we found you. You're safe now." He wiped tendrils of black hair from her face. When she raised her hand to touch his face, he noticed the bloody cuts. "We going to get you to a hospital."

Before she could answer, a cup appeared. She gulped down the contents, then smiled up at him. "I'm fine— really—just cold and hungry. Take me home, please."

"After a doctor checks you out. A couple of those cuts may need stitches."

She laid her head against his chest as he carried her from the building. TR and the superintendent cleared a path to the waiting ambulance. The electric-powered vehicle transported them to Bellevue Hospital, where a doctor and nurse stood waiting at the entrance. Tyler gently laid her on an exam table and stepped back. Chloe reached for his hand. "Don't leave me."

"I'm right here and I'm not going anywhere," he assured her.

The doctor did a cursory exam, cleaned and bandaged Chloe's hands, and announced her fit to go home. "You're one lucky lady." He looked up at Tyler. "You should make an appointment to see your own physician in about ten days to have the sutures taken out." He smiled and patted Chloe's shoulder. "We're all glad you're okay, Mrs. Reynolds."

By late afternoon, Tyler had her settled at home in bed. "Are you up to giving me a full account of what happened? Superintendent Devery is anxious to catch the thugs that did this to you." He touched a finger to Chloe's bandaged hand.

"Actually, I did that to myself. I was trying to cut the ropes with a piece of glass." She proceeded to tell her story while Tyler took notes.

"And you say you heard them mention bundles of money?"

"Yes, the boss man with the cigar wanted to make sure all the bundles were wrapped and hidden inside the bolts of fabric. I don't think they realized I could hear them. They must have been standing in the stairwell. Right before they left, they said they were coming back for me. They said something about a barrel and the harbor." She shuttered.

Tyler tapped the notebook against his leg. Everything Chloe said made sense after Tyler had talked to Devery and a few other members of the police force. Racketeering, extortion, and counterfeiting were becoming rampant in the boroughs, especially Little Italy. Chloe had probably stumbled onto one of their enterprises. *She's lucky they didn't kill her.*

"I need to get this information to Superintendent Devery. There's a guard posted outside and TR arranged for a nurse slash housekeeper. Her name is Molly O'Brien. You'll like her. She's an Irish version of Clare."

"Do you have to go?" She reached for him with bandaged hands.

Tyler fought the pleading in her eyes and leaned in to kiss her. His instincts told him there was more to this than children sewing buttons, and he needed to take care of it. *She doesn't fully understand the threat here.*

CHAPTER 16

Tyler arranged to have a tree delivered Christmas Eve morning, thinking decorating it would take Chloe's mind off what had happened to her. He hated to leave her, but he needed to ensure her safety. The only way he knew to do that was track down the lowlifes who had been operating the illegal sweatshop and moving money.

The meeting took place in the governor's office. Superintendent Devery blustered when Tyler asked to be included in the investigation. "Excuse me, Reynolds, but I don't remember ever pinning a New York City Police Officer's badge on your chest."

Tyler's temper raised a couple of notches. The man was obviously full of himself and liked to wield his power. He'd dealt with men like him before. "Sir, I have no intention of interfering with an ongoing investigation. I would merely like to be included when information comes in and will gladly share anything I find out that will put these scumbags behind bars."

Devery blustered. "Civilians have no business playing private detective."

TR waved a hand at the two men sitting across for him. "Okay, hold on a minute. Big Bill, you're obviously unaware that Tyler here is a former Pinkerton agent. He's trained in the latest investigation techniques. Take my word for it, this man is top notch. He wouldn't be working for me if he wasn't.

"His wife—the victim—has been a family friend since she was a child. I want this mess cleaned up satisfactory before I leave office. If that means you work together to make that happen then so be it."

He directed his attention to Tyler. "I'm also concerned for Chloe's safety. I'm giving you two weeks off, starting now, to gather enough evidence to catch these hooligans and put them behind bars. I understand a former associate of yours is acting as security while you're gone. Keep him on and send me the bill."

When Tyler started to protest, Roosevelt held up his hand. "Let me finish. This is not up for discussion. Besides Oliver being a good and faithful friend for many years, Chloe's father provided my men and me with the weaponry necessary to keep us alive in Cuba. I owe him a huge debt of gratitude, and this is my way of repaying that debt."

Tyler stood and extended his hand. "Thank you, sir, for… well, for everything. I'll keep you informed of my progress."

❦

Devery escort Tyler into the precinct and up to Captain Boyle's office. The captain rose from behind his desk with a sigh and an irritated scowl. "I just got a call from the governor's office. Seems you, Mr. Reynolds, have more clout than Superintendent Devery or I realized. But—just so you understand—I don't care what kind of training you've had or who you worked for. This is my investigation. Is that clear?"

Tyler clinched his teeth and let out a slow breath through his nose to calm himself. He didn't have time to play stupid, macho games, but he also didn't want to step on anyone's toes, especially if he might need them later. He forced a smile. "Gentlemen, I assure you, you won't even know I'm around. So I can be up to speed, I'd like access to any profiles you may have for organized gangs and crime families, specifically ones that are known to work out of the garment district and Little Italy."

Boyle bristled. "Those files do not leave these premises, understand?"

Tyler shrugged. "Fine. Give me a desk somewhere and I'll study them here."

Three hours later he was stretching the ache out of his back in the tiny closet they relegated him to. He'd learned everything he needed to know about the illegal enterprises happening in the city. *I'll be glad when we get out of here.* He didn't want Chloe exposed to any more danger or the seedy underworld that seemed to be getting a strong grip on the metropolis.

In a bathroom, he changed out of the suit he had been wearing and donned worn workman's clothes he stashed in an equally worn carpet bag. Standing in front of a mirror, he appraised his reflection. The clothes worked. He ran a hand over the dark stubble that covered the lower half of his face and wished he had more time to let his beard grow out. Running his fingers through his wavy auburn hair, pulled it out of its carefully combed style and allowed the natural curl to take over. *That looks better.* He doffed a flat newsboy's cap and pulled the brim forward to conceal his eyes.

Strolling through the neighborhood where they found Chloe, Tyler acted like he belonged. He stopped and engaged shop owners and residents along the way in conversation. Most were friendly and unknowingly supplied him with tidbits of useful information.

He went back to the alleyway, where they found the door leading to Chloe. Leaning against the brick wall, he wrote down specifics of what he'd learned in a small pocket notebook.

"Hey, you're the guy from yesterday." The boy looked him up and down. "Playin' poor, are ya?" He grinned. "Smart. People around here will talk easier to their own kind than to some fancy pants rich bloke."

Kid's sharp. Maybe I can use him. Tyler stayed where he was. "Think so, huh? What's your name?"

"Henry. Everyone calls me Hank or Two Bits though 'cause I'll do just about anything for two bits." The boy nodded his chin in Tyler's direction. "What's yours? Figure it's fake. Still, I gotta call you somethun."

"You can call me Trace for now." Tyler put the notebook and pencil away. "Not going to sell many papers this time of day on Christmas Eve. How about I buy the ones you have left and we go to your place to talk? I'd kind of like to get out of this cold and warm up a bit."

Hank twisted his mouth from one side to the other in indecision, then jerked his head. "Follow me."

Tyler trailed after the boy. He knew the kid was probably older than he looked, knowing his diet was sure to be wholly inadequate for a growing child. He had dirty blonde hair that curled at the nap of his equally dirty neck. A spatter of freckles crossed the bridge of a finely shaped nose and lay across his chapped red cheeks. He had dark-lashed gray eyes the color of a stormy sky. *If he survives, he'll be a handsome man someday.*

They stepped down a short flight of concrete stairs. Hank produced a key and opened the lock on a stout metal door. "Can't be too careful in this neighborhood."

Light filtered around a board covering a small, grimy window at street level. Tyler could see they had come into the cramped boiler room for the building above them. A lumpy pile of bedding took up one corner closest to the rusted old boiler. Several crates served as a table and cupboard for his meager belongings and a couple of tins of food.

The boy lit a stub of candle and plopped down on his homemade bed. "So, I figure you're back to find the blackguards who hurt that pretty lady. She your wife, or sister, maybe?"

Tyler settled onto a rickety chair with wire securing the front two legs together and debated how much to divulge to the lad. "My wife. Where did you pick up a word like blackguards?"

Hank crawled over to the crate and pulled out a ragged stack of magazines. He grabbed up the top one and showed it to Tyler. It was an old copy of 'The Strand'. "I can read," Hank replied with a proud tilt to his chin. "I like all the stuff about Sherlock Holmes the best."

Tyler suppressed a smile and tried to look as serious as the lad. "I see. I've always enjoyed Sir Arthur Conan Doyle myself. Man is a skilled storyteller." Tyler rubbed his chin as if in deep thought. "So tell me, Hank, do you think you'd make a good detective?"

The boy sat up straight. "You bet ya. You needin' an assistant like Sherlock? I could be your Doctor Watson."

Tyler laughed. "I'll bet you'd make a great Watson." He looked at the kid's hopeful face. There was something there that reminded him of himself at that awkward age. "Just how old are you, Hank?"

The boy ducked his head as if ashamed or embarrassed. "I know I don't look it, but I'm thirteen, well almost." Then he brought up his chin and gave Tyler a hard look. "I've been on my own and doing just fine for three years now. Selling papers and running errands gets me by. I got no fancy education. Taught myself 'cipherin' and I can read and write real good too. Someday I want to be a famous writer. You think that's possible, Mr. Trace?"

It surprised Tyler that the kid had managed to survive on his own for so long. There was no doubt he was resourceful and smart. "My dad always said it was important for a man to have a dream, something to shoot for. You work at it, build your skills and anything is possible." He got up. "Tell you what; you can be my assistant on this investigation. I'll pay you twenty-five cents a day so you won't have to sell newspapers or run errands. Deal?"

Henry joined him and stretched out a grubby hand. "Just call me Doctor Watson."

"Well, okay Doc. I say we get started. First, I want to check out the building next door."

"Lookin' for clues, right?"

Tyler grabbed his bag and headed for the door. "Exactly. We need to figure out who those scoundrels are so we can track them down."

It was getting late. Chloe would be worried about him, so Tyler decided to call it a day. Their search of the abandon building only gave them one small clue—a scrap of paper with what looked like Italian written on it. He'd need to find someone who could decipher it for him, and on Christmas Eve that would be near to impossible.

He looked at Hank. The boy was so skinny his too short trousers gaped at the waist and had to be held up by a pair of ratty suspenders. *I can't send him back to that hovel, especially on Christmas Eve.*

"Hank, my man, how would you like to accompany me home? I'm sure my wife would love to meet my new assistant." *I hope this doesn't come back to bite me.*

The boy's expression changed for hopeful surprise to resigned disappointment. "I can't. I don't have me no nice clothes to wear and besides—in case you hadn't noticed—I stink. Gettin' a bath is near impossible around here."

Tyler kept a serious look on his own face. "I happen to own a bathtub and I'll bet we can even find you some clean clothes." He draped his arm across the boy's thin shoulders. "Come on, it's no fun spending Christmas Eve alone. There's my wife's chocolate cake to consider. It's probably the best I've ever tasted."

Tyler knew he had him. The kid was almost salivating at the mere thought of the sweet dessert.

CHAPTER 17

Chloe stood back and admired her handiwork. The tree looked beautiful. Setting in the bowed front window, it presented a cheery sight for passersby. She wouldn't light the tiny candles in their holders until Tyler came home so they could do it together. *Our first Christmas*. It was also her first Christmas without the Morrisons. *I wonder if Auntie Clare and Abel miss me as much as I miss them?* Before she had a chance to carry that thought any farther, she heard a key rattle the front doorknob.

"I'll get that. You stay put." Andrew ordered as he lumbered from the room.

Chloe liked Tyler's best friend, but having him underfoot all day had been disconcerting. She was glad her husband was home to relieve him of guard duty. Molly, the nurse Uncle Teedie hired, had already gone home to be with her own family for Christmas Eve.

Chloe smiled in anticipation, hoping her decorating skills would impress her husband. She waited patiently in the parlor, as instructed. She could hear the men talking in low voices in the entry hall. When she heard them coming, she positioned herself in front of the tree with her back to the archway. "Ta-da! What do you think?"

"Wow, that's the prettiest tree I've ever seen."

The unfamiliar voice of a child turned Chloe around to find a street urchin standing in her parlor with Tyler and Andrew positioned behind the boy. Tyler's hand rested on a narrow shoulder. "Chloe, I'd like you to meet my new assistant, Henry..."

"Henry Alonzo Perkins. Please to meet you, ma'am." He wiped his palm on his threadbare coat and extended it politely. "Most everybody calls me Two Bits or Hank."

Chloe gathered herself and smiled. "Welcome, Henry." She shook his hand. He stared at her with big gray-blue eyes. Flustered, she wiped at her cheek. "Do I have something on my face?"

"No, ma'am. It's just you're even prettier up close. Even prettier than my ma before she got sick. She was a real beauty according to my pa."

Chloe blushed. Even from a grungy little kid, the compliment was nice. "Why thank you, Henry." She looked at Tyler for guidance.

Picking up her cue, he announced, "Hank, here, is going to stay with us a couple of days since we're working so closely together. He could use a bath and clean clothes so I'll take him upstairs and we'll get cleaned up before dinner."

Chloe could see the uncertainty on the boy's face and wanted to make him feel welcomed. "It looks like we're having a dinner party. I've invited Andrew to stay as well."

Andrew huffed. "Not like you could get me to leave without some of that delicious-looking chocolate cake I spied in the kitchen."

Chloe saw Tyler secret some money to Andrew and whisper something to him before marching young Henry up the stairs. The big man grinned and headed to the front door. "I have an errand to run before the stores close. Hold supper for me, I'll be back."

She was relieved Tyler saw the need for some new clothes for their guest. He certainly had nothing that would fit, and even though she wasn't much taller than Henry, she had a lot more curves. Assured the men could handle things, Chloe headed to the kitchen to check on the pot roast Molly had in the oven.

When Tyler and Henry joined her a half hour later, it startled her to see the change in their young guest. His scrubbed face rosy, his hair a soft shade of blonde, he was wearing one of Tyler's shirts with the sleeves rolled up. Chloe spied a pair of knobby knees before looking away so as not to embarrass the boy. "I hope you two are hungry. This is just about ready." She smiled at Henry. "Since you're our guest, I'll let you decide where we eat, in here or the dining room."

Henry peeked into the formal room beyond the archway and back at the large rectory table in the center of the kitchen. "I like in here better. I'm not used to fancy."

"What say we help Miss Chloe out and get it set then?" Tyler moved to the rack above the sideboard and started pulling down plates just as the doorbell rang. "I'll get it. Hank, the silverware is in the drawer there. I'll be right back."

Chloe hoped it was Andrew back from his mission. Supper could wait long enough for Henry to change into some clothes that fit him. She watched the boy trying to figure out where the forks and spoons went. "One on either side will work just fine. Thank you for your help."

Henry gave her a shy grin, the rose in his cheeks turning a deeper shade of pink. "You're welcome, Miss Chloe."

She smiled. *This is going to be a very different kind of Christmas than I expected.*

❧❧

Tyler answered the door to find Andrew standing there with his arms full. "Did you buy out the store?"

"I tried. The owner was shutting the doors early, so I grabbed what I could. I hope something in here fits."

The two men arranged the packages around the base of the tree. "Let's light the candles and then call them in."

Satisfied everything looked good, and they hadn't missed a candle, Tyler called out, "Chloe, Hank, could you come in here, please."

As soon as Hank stepped into the room, the two men broke out in a chorus of 'O Christmas Tree'.

The boy's eyes rounded in wonder at the lighted tree. "Wow, that's somethin', ain't it Miss Chloe." He turned and smiled up at her.

Tyler couldn't mistake the adoration in his eyes. *I'd better be careful or he'll be stealing my woman.* "I think there're some presents here that might be of interest to you, my man." He motioned Hank closer, eager to see the boy's reaction to his gifts.

Henry dropped to his knees and picked up a brown paper-wrapped bundle. "For me? Really?"

Chloe settled into a chair. "Hurry and open them. I want to see too."

He ripped into the packages, sending paper and twine flying. "Look," he cried in awe and held up a blue wool coat. In another bundle, he found a hat, gloves, and scarf. The next two held worsted trousers, shirts, drawers, and socks. He gave Chloe an embarrassed look and quickly tucked the underwear out of sight.

Andrew chuckled. "Can't be letting the ladies see a man's knickers." He pulled a box from behind his back. "Here's one last box."

Henry held it with reverence and rubbed a hand over the printed picture of a pair of black boots. With reluctance and sorrow written all over his face, he handed the box back. "This is too much. A man shouldn't take charity."

Andrew pushed it back at him. "This isn't charity, son. It's Christmas—time for giving presents and spreading cheer. Isn't that right, Tyler?"

Tyler patted the boy's shoulder, then gave it a squeeze. "Sure is. Not accepting a gift isn't polite. Besides, I think you'd look better in something your own size, don't you?"

Henry chewed his lip in thought, then gave each of the adults a smile and held up the boots. "Can I try them on?"

"Only after you put the rest of your new clothes on first." Andrew chuckled.

Henry dashed from the room, his arms loaded down with his store-bought finery.

"And hurry up. I'm hungry," called Tyler after him.

After getting the boy tucked in for the night, Tyler and Chloe crept across the hall to the third bedroom. Stacked inside were the contents of the Philadelphia house Chloe couldn't make herself part with.

"It's here somewhere." She stood on tiptoe to see over the crates, boxes, and furniture piled throughout the room. "There!" She clapped her hands and wiggled her way to a large camel-backed steamer trunk.

Before Tyler could reach her, she was working through a set of different sized keys dangling from a round ring. "Here, let me." He kneeled beside her and pushed the smallest of the keys into the lock. The latch sprang open with a twist of his wrist.

On top, in folds of tissue, lay Chloe's wedding dress and veil. With a reverence reserved for holy things, Tyler watched her lift it out. "Here, hold this. I don't want to take a chance on getting it dirty."

Below her dress was an assortment of albums, bric-à-brac, and memorabilia. Chloe pulled things out and set them on the floor around them. "It's got to be here somewhere. I remember Auntie Clare saying she put it away in this trunk for safekeeping." She bent double over the side to reach the bottom, her derriere pointed skyward.

Tyler smiled and shook his head. "Take your time. I'm admiring the view."

She squealed in triumph and came up out of the depths of the trunk, holding a wooden case the size of a large serving tray. Puffing strands of hair out of her face, she held up her find. "Papa gave me this when I turned thirteen. It's ten years old. I hope the paints are still good."

Together, they reloaded the chest with its treasures and quietly made their way back down the stairs. Diverting to the kitchen, Chloe laid the wooden box on the table and opened it. Nestled inside were an assortment of brushes, graphite pencils, charcoal sticks, and tubes of paints. A palette with faded splotches of color on it, a small easel, and a stack of stiff paper were strapped to the inside cover.

"This hardly looks used." Tyler lifted out the paper and uncovered a finished painting. The colors had lost their vibrancy, but he could still see the subject was an orange tabby cat curled on a rug in front of a fireplace. At a loss for words, he muttered an inoffensive "oh" then tried to cover himself. "It's Magic, right?"

"The first Magic." She grabbed the canvas out of his hands. "And yes, I know. I have no talent. I figured that out right away." She studied the painting and frowned. "I wanted to be as famous as Monet or Renoir."

Tyler took the canvas back and turned it sideways. "It looks other worldly and kind of disjointed." He shrugged his shoulders. "I say we keep it. Who knows, maybe someday this kind of art will be in vogue."

Chloe punched him in the arm and stuck out her tongue. "You better be careful, mister, or I'll take back your presents."

CHAPTER 18

Christmas proved to be an unexpected delight. Chloe was sure she'd be feeling blue since Clare and Abel weren't there on her second Christmas without her father. Having young Henry in the house added a certain gay frivolity she hadn't experienced since she was a child herself.

Forbidding Molly to come in on Christmas, she was on her own in the kitchen and enjoying herself immensely. The turkey was all ready to go into the oven and a pecan pie cooled on the windowsill. She suppressed a cough with the back of her bandaged hand and turned a flapjack over when Tyler came up behind her. "Merry Christmas, my lovely wife." He wrapped his arms around her and nuzzled her neck.

"Ah, damn, are you mugging her?"

Tyler and Chloe both turned to find Henry standing in the doorway.

With a stern look on his face, Tyler shook a finger at him. "Watch your mouth, young man, there's a lady present."

The boy lowered his head and mumbled. "Sorry."

Not wanting to spoil the morning, Chloe smiled and ignored the exchange. "I hope you like pancakes. I've got scrambled eggs on the warmer and the sausage is done, so you two sit yourselves down. Tyler, could you get the milk out of the icebox, please?"

"Who's Tyler?" Henry asked.

Chloe piled a stack of pancakes on the plate in front of him. "Why, that's Tyler." She laughed and pointed the spatula.

Tyler joined them and set the jug in the middle of the table. "Trace was my undercover name when I was a detective at Pinkertons."

Henry shoveled a forkful of pancake into his mouth and spoke around it. "You were a real hawkshaw like Sherlock?"

Chloe gave Tyler a scowl. "That was a long time ago." Looking down at the eggs on the plate she handed to Tyler, she suddenly felt queasy. "Excuse me, please."

Trying not to cause alarm, she walked from the room, then dashed up the stairs to the washroom. Not having eaten yet, there wasn't much to bring up. When the stomach spasms subsided, Chloe pulled herself off the floor and washed her face. Her pale reflection stared back at her. "What was that all about?" she asked her image.

She did a quick rinse of her mouth and headed back downstairs. A spasm of coughing stopped her halfway. Must be getting a cold. Maybe that would account for the tiredness she had been feeling lately.

Chloe stopped short of the kitchen doorway, took a deep breath, and let it out. Tyler and Henry laughed over some shared secret. When she entered the room, her husband's face moved from happy to concerned in an instant. *Do I look that bad?*

He set his plate down and came to her side. "What's wrong? Are you ill? Here, sit down." He pulled a chair out and lowered her gently to the seat. "Let me get you some water."

Chloe waved her hand. "I'm fine, really. Leave the dishes for now. Let's open presents." She clapped her hands and smiled with enthusiasm.

Taking her cue, Tyler rubbed his hands together. "I can't wait to see what Santa brought me." He turned to Henry. "How about you?"

The boy shrugged his shoulders and tried to look disinterested. Chloe could see it was a struggle for him to act so nonchalant. He probably hasn't had a real Christmas in a while.

"Come on, let's check under the tree." Tyler went around and dragged the boy to his feet and out of the room, giving her time to ease out of the chair and put on a bright face.

Below the large spruce, a small assortment of packages waited. Chloe gained the side chair, glad to sit and allow her stomach time to settle. "Henry, would you do the honors and pass the gifts out?"

"Sure," he replied, felling to his knees. He picked up a small box wrapped in red tissue paper and a piece of green ribbon. "The tag says 'To my wonderful husband'. That's you, right?"

"That's me, Mr. Wonderful."

Chloe was next. He pushed a large square box to her feet, the brown paper wrapping giving nothing away. "That's all of them."

Chloe stifled a grin as she watched Tyler put on a confused look. Like an excited child, he got down on the floor and looked under the lowest branches. *He's really enjoying himself. He'll make a great father someday.*

"That's not right." He huffed. "Surely he didn't forget you. Wait, I think I see something. I think you'd better hunker down and looked way back under the tree."

Henry dropped and belly crawl under the bottom boughs. Tyler grinned and gave her a wink. "See anything?"

There was a muffled gasp. "Yeah, it's big!" Seconds later, Henry was scooting back out, pulling a couple of gaily wrapped packages with him, his expression priceless. A mix of wonder and disbelief replaced his normal look of cool indifference. "They have my name on them!"

Chloe laughed. "Well, then I guess you'd better open them."

Tyler came to sit on the arm of her chair and entwined his fingers with hers. They both watched in anticipation as Henry tore the wrappings away.

The boy's eyes rounded along with his mouth. He looked from the art case to Tyler and Chloe. "Golly, a genuine artist's case." He rubbed his palms over the wooden top in reverence.

"Open it. Let's see what's inside." Tyler let go of her hand and dropped to sprawl on the floor next to Henry. In minutes, they had everything spread out on the rug around them and were examining each brush and pencil.

"Hey, you forgot one." Chloe pointed to the unopened present behind Henry.

The tissue unfolded to reveal a stack of notepads and a box of pencils she'd bought for Tyler a month earlier. She looked at him with a raised eyebrow.

Tyler shrugged. "Hank wants to be a writer. I guess Santa must have figured that out."

Henry sat back on his heels. "This is the best Christmas I've ever had." He jumped up to give Chloe an awkward hug and whispered in her ear. "Don't tell Mr. Tyler, but I don't believe in Santa Claus."

CHAPTER 19

Tyler woke to find Chloe's side of the bed empty. The pewter-gray light peeking between the drapes confirmed the early hour—too early for her to be up. Concerned, he climbed out of bed, pulled on his robe, and padded out to the hall. Faint light shone beneath the bathroom door. Remembering her upset stomach from the day before, he tapped and whispered into the wood panel. "Chloe, darling, are you okay?"

"I'm fine. I'll be right out."

Tyler didn't know how to help. He needed to do something. "Do you want me to start breakfast?" The sound of a snort carried through the door. "Hey, I'll have you know I can crack an egg with the best of them."

The door opened. "I'll just bet you can." Chloe's pale face smiled up at him.

"You don't look so good."

She brushed a long tentacle of raven-black hair off her cheek. "Must be a stomach bug or something." She wrapped her arms around his waist and looked up at him. "It's early. If you're not afraid I'll contaminate you, we could both go back to bed, and I'll show you how much I love my new camera."

Tyler gathered her up in his arms. "Sounds like a good way to say 'thank you' to me." He carried her down the hall.

"I know we can't afford it, but I'm glad you bought it for me. I need to finish getting the rest of the photographs I need for the child labor article."

Tyler's back stiffened. "Whoa. You can't go back down to the district after what happened."

Chloe's arms dropped away from their hold around his neck. "I don't see why not. My hands will be fine and I'll feel better tomorrow."

Tyler felt his temper rise along with a mix of worry and admiration. He had to stop her. She didn't understand how much danger she was still in. He couldn't think with her in his arms and lowered her to the floor to give himself time and space to come up with a convincing argument. "You know, the Bible says a wife is supposed to submit to her husband."

Chloe's face went from alabaster pale to angry red. She jutted out her chin and wagged a finger at him. "Don't you dare throw the Bible at me. I don't intend to hide away like some mouse scurrying back to its hole afraid of the big, bad cat." She stomped into their bedroom and turned at the door. "I have a job to do and I intend to finish it." She slammed the door before he could stop her.

"So much for putting down my foot." He rubbed the back of his neck and turned to find Hank looking at him from the threshold of his own room. "She's mad, huh?"

"Yeah, you could say that. Let me give you a piece of advice. Never tell a woman she can't, especially stubborn ones." Tyler looked back at the closed door. This wasn't over. He'd make sure she stayed put if he had to hogtie her to the bedpost.

"I guess we're on our own for breakfast, huh?"

Tyler snorted a laugh, remembering how important food was to a growing boy, especially one who didn't get much. "I guess so. Might as well get dressed and meet me downstairs. We'll see what we can rustle up."

When Hank joined him in the kitchen, the boy seemed subdued. Tyler worked to draw him out. "So you ready to play detective, Mr. Watson?"

Hank shrugged and wiped up egg yolk with a piece of half-eaten toast. "I guess so." He finished his milk and swiped an arm across his mouth. "You ain't plannin' on going out like that, are ya?"

Tyler gulped down the last of his coffee. "Let me get changed and we'll go."

He climbed the stairs and stopped in front of the bedroom door. Quietly, he tried the doorknob, surprised when it turned in his hand. Cautious of flying objects, he peeked into the darkened bedroom. Chloe was asleep. The covers pulled up and clutched in one hand. Good. I'm not ready to do battle again. He grabbed some clothes and headed to the bathroom.

When he came back down, Hank was sitting on the bottom step, his new art kit, tablets, and box of pencils beside him. Tyler recognized the tattered gray coat, its sleeves tied together to hold his old clothes inside. His holey, worn-out boots hung by the laces over his thin shoulder.

"What's going on?" He eased down beside the boy, allowing his bad leg to jut out and rest on the floor.

Hank squared his shoulders and started gathering up his belongings. "Nothing. Just waitin' on you to take me home."

Tyler pushed the boy back down when he started to stand. "Did something change I don't know about?"

Hank wouldn't look at him. Instead, he fiddled with his shoelaces. "Just figured I've worn out my welcome. Miss Chloe might not be so mad at you if I'm not around. 'sides, I need to get back to my papers before some other newsie steals my corner and Mr. Jeffers gives my room away."

"I see. So staying here isn't working out for you, huh? Don't like my cooking? Bed to lumpy?"

Hank gave him a sidelong look, like he was crazy. "Miss Chloe's the best cook in the country. You're not bad, but she's world class." He pressed his fingers together and blew a kiss off the ends of them like some Italian connoisseur. "And that bed is like sleepin' on a cloud. Done thought I'd gone to heaven or somethun." His face sobered. "You and the missus have been real nice, but I'm just a street kid. I don't belong in a place like this. Figure I'd best get back to my own neighborhood before I get to comfortable."

Tyler could see the tough kid act was little more than a facade. *He's afraid of being rejected.* He hadn't considered what would happen once Christmas was over. It was obvious the kid needed someone to care about him and give him a home. He thought about his own parents. If he had been younger when they were killed, he could have found himself in Hank's shoes, alone and on his own. The thought made him cringe. *What would I have turned out like if I'd been on my own like Hank?*

He wrapped an arm around the boy's shoulders. "My man, I think you and I need each other. I mean, what's Holmes without Watson? We're a team and teams stick together. If you're willing to give up having your own place and the newspaper business, I'd sure appreciate it if you'd consider staying on here. I know it won't be easy. Once a man's been on his own, it's kinda hard to give up your freedom, but I promise, Miss Chloe and I will try not to make it too rough on you. What do you say? Willing to give it a try?"

Hank searched Tyler's face. "You really mean it? I can stay here with you and Miss Chloe and eat regular like?"

It was a decision he should have made with her, but now that he was in, he couldn't back out. "Yes, I mean it. I have to warn you though; they'll be house rules you'll have to follow just like me."

Hank chuckled. "Yeah, I wouldn't want to make Miss Chloe mad like you did this morning. She's fearsome when she's riled."

Tyler tousled the boy's hair and got to his feet. "You want to know a secret? She scares me, too, sometimes." He looked back up the stairs. *I hope you don't kill me for this one.*

The doorbell rang.

"Go put your stuff away while I see who this is." He swung the door open to Andrew's big frame blocking the winter sun.

"I figured you'd want to get an early start."

Tyler snorted. "You were hoping for breakfast, admit it."

Andrew tried to act offended, then laughed. "You're one luck man, Reynolds."

"You wouldn't think so today. I'm afraid the only breakfast left is cold eggs and toast I had to whip up myself this morning." He glanced up the stairs. "Chloe's sick, and she's angry with me at the moment. I'm hoping she'll spend the day in bed." He ran a hand through his damp hair. "Listen, whatever you do, don't let her leave this house, understand?" He felt guilty for the battle Andrew would face later.

The giant clicked his heels and saluted. "Yes, sir." He relaxed his stance. "You didn't forbid her to leave, did you?"

Tyler plopped his hat down on his head. "What if I did? I'm her husband. I'm just looking out for her best interests."

Andrew chuckled and wagged his massive head. "I thought you learned that lesson already. You must be slow, son."

"Mr. Tyler's not slow. He's a detective like Sherlock Holmes." Hank informed the big man as he came down the stairs to join them. "Detectives have to be real smart and cunning to find all the clues and solve the case. Right, Mr. Tyler?"

Tyler ignored the smirk on Andrew's face. "That's right. Here, put the rest of your new winter gear on and let's go so Mr. Andrew can do his babysitting duties." He winked at his friend over the boy's head. "Molly should be here shortly. I'm sure she wouldn't mind fixing you some breakfast. We've got a crime to solve."

CHAPTER 20

Tyler walked along beside Hank, the frosty morning air crystallizing every breath and making the tips of their noses cherry red. It was early enough that most of the businesses weren't open yet, including the tailor and bookmaker in Little Italy. "Where's this grocer you told me about?"

"Mr. Rossi's store is just across the street over there." Hank pointed a gloved hand down the block. "He speaks pretty good English, but he's real good at Italian, especially when he's yelling."

"And you know this because you've given him cause to yell at you?"

Hank shrugged a shoulder and ducked his head. "Only a couple of times when he thought I stole somethun."

Tyler gave him a stern look. "That's something we'll have to have a serious talk about." He held the shop door open and let Hank duck in under his arm. "Right now, we need to be sharp. Listen and watch for any clues. You never know what might end up being important."

Hank made the introductions. Mr. Rossi wiped a pudgy hand on his apron and shook hands. "Buongiorno. Ah, gooda mornun. How canna I helpa you today?"

Tyler passed the grocer the slip of paper with the Italian writing. "We found this and were hoping you could tell us what it says."

The chubby old man silently mouthed the words. His face went from friendly and animated to closed and frightened. "Mi dispiace non posso aiutarti. Sorry, I canna not helpa you." He shook his head and pushed the paper scrap back at Tyler as if it was on fire.

Unwilling to give up so easily, Tyler ignored the paper and pressed the man. "You can't or you won't? Is someone putting pressure on you?"

The shopkeeper pleaded with his hands. "Per cortesia, I donna want any trouble."

The man's poorly disguised fear was all the answer Tyler needed. Somebody had already gotten to him. He didn't want to bring any trouble down on the man, so he took the scrawled message back and they left without argument.

"Where we goin' now?" Hank trotted to keep up with Tyler's long stride.

"To the police station."

Hank skidded to a stop. "Do we have to? I don't have much use for coppers."

Tyler's day hadn't gone well so far, and he wasn't in any mood to argue. "Fine, go back to your room. I'll take care of this alone and meet you there in an hour."

"You're not mad, are ya?"

Tyler stopped and looked back to where Hank stood, looking forlorn and uncertain. "No, kid, just go. I'll see you in a while."

The police station was busy. Tyler waited outside Captain Boyle's office, tapping his foot and twirling his hat. Impatiently, he snapped his watch open for the third time. The man had kept him waiting for eight minutes. So far, the day had produced nothing. He hoped the captain had good news.

"Reynolds, come in." Boyle shouted from inside the office.

Tyler dropped the watch back in his pocket and checked his attitude. It wouldn't do any good to antagonize the man. "Captain, hope you had a nice Christmas." Without waiting for a reply, he continued as he dropped into a chair opposite the officer. "I found a scrap of paper in the tenement where they held my wife. It appears to be in Italian. Do you have someone who can translate it?"

Boyle gave him a scowl from under his bushy eyebrows. "Giordano," he bellowed. "Get yourself in here."

A young, good-looking officer sauntered into the room. "Yeah, Captain?"

"You're a dago, right?"

"And proud of it." The cop rested his hands on his hips.

The captain jerked his chin at the paper in Tyler's hand. "Read that."

Giordano took the paper and read it over. "Don't make much sense with the paper torn like that. From what I figure, this is a date: December twenty-six, midnight. Hey, that's today! And this here says Ferry Street docks, then there's something about the naked lady or maybe that's naked lily, belladonna nudo. It's hard to make out." He shook his head and handed the slip back to Tyler. "I think those are dollar signs." He pointed to several squiggly symbols.

Tyler's instincts told him they were on to something. "Could you call the Port Authority and get a list of all incoming ships flying an Italian flag?"

Boyle's bushy eyebrows drew together. He opened his mouth to say something, then changed his mind and picked up the phone. His half of the conversation was direct and abrupt. He dropped the receiver back on the hook. "It'll be here within the hour." The man tilted back in his chair, his scowl deepened. "We haven't been sitting on our hands, Reynolds. You should know we think this all has to do with the Costa Nostra. You're heard of the Sicilian Mafia?"

Tyler shook his head. A new sense of dread crept in.

"Well, they're becoming a presence here in the US. We suspect one particular group; The Hundred and Seventh Street Mob has moved in and been working the district. Their boss is a guy name Giuseppe 'The Clutch Hand' Morello. They're into extortion, loan-sharking, robbery, and counterfeiting using sweatshops as fronts to launder money."

Tyler sat forward. "Sounds like an ugly group of thugs. Dangerous?"

"Very. That's why we're taking this so seriously." Boyle also leaned forward and rested his forearms on the desk. "You're lucky your wife is still in one piece—literally."

Tyler's stomach twisted at the implication. "There was a lot more than luck involved. Will they come after her?"

Boyle and Tyler both stood as a woman brought in a shaft of papers and handed them to him. He read through each page, then let the stack fall to his desk. "There's a cargo ship due in tonight called the SS Belladonna Spoglio. It will be docking at the piers on Ferry Street."

Tyler crossed his arms. "You didn't answer my question. Will they come after her?"

Boyle swiped a hand across his forehead. "Probably. They don't like witnesses."

"Then our best bet is to get to them before they can get to her. Can I use your phone?" Tyler didn't wait for his consent. He had the operator connect him to the brownstone. Andrew answered.

"Andy, I need you to get a couple more men guarding the house. Don't say anything to Chloe, I don't want to alarm her."

"That bad, huh? I'll make the call as soon as we hang up."

"How is she?" Tyler remembered back to the bout of vomiting she'd had that morning and felt guilty for his part in their argument. *I'd better apologize and make sure she's okay.* He also wanted to ask her if either of her captors had a deformed hand. "Can you put her on, please?"

Tyler waited for what seemed like forever. When Andrew came back on the line, his voice was low and strained. "Tyler, she's not there. She's been up in your room all day—sleeping mostly from what Molly says. Now she's gone. I checked the rest of the house. Chloe's not here. I'm sorry, man. I don't know how she did it, but she most of snuck out."

Tyler's heart seemed to stop then pound in his chest. He didn't know whether to be angry or scared to death. "I've got to go. Start a search from your end. Contact the fourteenth precinct if you find her."

Before Andrew could reply, Tyler hung up. He looked at Boyle. "They may already have her."

CHAPTER 21

Tyler spent the rest of the day chasing shadows. At one point, he and Boyle were called to the dead end of a cramped alley. A group of uniform-clad cops parted as the two men walked up. An eager, wide-eyed young officer stepped forward. "Looks like a woman, boss. We haven't touched nothing. Went by the book just like you said."

Tyler's gut twisted. All the air in his lungs rushed out at the sight of two impossibly small feet protruding from under a piece of rusted corrugated sheet metal. "Chloe! My God, no!" He pushed forward and fell to his knees. Before anyone could stop him, he lifted the scrap of steel and threw it aside. Beneath the makeshift grave lay the half-clothed body of a woman. Long brown hair partially hid her face. Blood covered the expanse of her torso. One hand lay over the stomach wound as if she were trying to squelch the flow as her life ebbed from her. Vacant green eyes stared at the sky.

He sat back on his heels. His hand shook as he brought it up to cover his mouth. He closed his eyes and fought the sob that threatened to escape. A hand came down on his hunched shoulder and squeezed. He looked up at the captain, trying to suppress the guilty feeling of relief that coursed through his body. "It's not her. It's not my Chloe."

FRAGILE REPRIEVE

❧❧

Night fell. Throughout the long afternoon, Tyler had checked in with Andrew and Molly—their search as empty as his own. His desperation mounted until he felt like he would explode if something didn't break soon.

Now it was past midnight. The two squads of men hidden among the crates stacked along the wharf remained invisible. A tug positioned on either side guided the large ship they were waiting for into port. This was it. It had to go down as planned. Whatever was on that ship could be the bargaining chip that could save Chloe's life.

No one moved when two freight wagons pulled up to the gangplank. They needed to catch them in the act of transferring whatever illegal contraband the ship was transporting. Boyle and Tyler agreed it was probably counterfeit money, two large wagons worth. The team from the wagons moved swiftly, hauling crates from the ship's deck to the waiting drays.

Tyler watched from his position as two men, one with his arm in a sling, stood off to the side, directing the unloading. *Those are the ringleaders. I need to focus on them.*

He allowed the hate to rise in him to give himself strength. He really needed a gun if he wanted to get their attention and keep it, but Boyle refused to give him one. Tyler pulled the derringer from his waistband and gave it a critical look. It was Oliver Cantrell's own double barrel rimfire design and shot a thirty-eight caliber cartridge that was deadly at four yards or less. The problem was, he'd have to get close enough or risk missing his target, and he needed one of them alive to tell him where they were keeping Chloe.

Tyler waited until the duo were distracted and moved in closer. The single overhead electric light wasn't nearly sufficient to cover the whole dockside area. Still, it allowed him to get a better look at the men overseeing the unloading. Both were dark-haired and mustached. The larger of the two looked dangerous and mean, just like Chloe described him. He flicked the ash from the stub of a cigar. The other could have been any young emigrant except for the deformed hand he wore in a sling. That was definitely Morello, the crime boss of the Hundred and Seventh Street Mob.

The last crate was loaded, and still Boyle didn't give the signal. *What's he waiting for?* Tyler was getting impatient.

A shout came from the captain's direction. "Police! You're surrounded. Drop your weapons and get on the ground. Now!"

Pandemonium broke out. A dozen men scattered and were pursued. Tyler never let his eyes leave his targets. He sprang from behind the crate, his gun out at arm's length. "Morello, you're under arrest. Both of you get your hands in the air."

As the smaller man raised his one good hand, the brute beside him tossed his cigar and knocked him off balance. He turned and ran into the shadows of a giant warehouse. Tyler didn't let the sudden commotion distract him. He fired after the fugitive. The man was too far away for the bullet to reach his target, yet he went down hard and laid still.

Boyle moved into the light from the other side. Tyler could see a waft of hot smoke rise from his gun barrel in the cold night air. Morello stood there, one hand raised and a smile on his face. Tyler only had a second to contemplate why the man seemed so unconcerned before pain and darkness blacked out his world.

CHAPTER 22

Chloe staggered from the carriage. She would have fallen had the hack not jumped from his seat and caught her. "Thank you. Could you hand me my satchel, please?"

"Surely, ma'am. Let me carry it for you. Here, take my arm." The stocky driver shouldered her bag and extended his arm for support. "Let me just get you to the door."

Together they managed the steps leading up to the brownstone's entrance. It flew open before Chloe could get out her key. Molly gasped, one hand splayed across her chest. "Miss Chloe, you gave us such a fright. Andrew is beside himself. He's got a bunch of men out scouring the neighborhood for you." She stepped back and allowed the cabby to guide her inside.

Chloe handed Molly her clasp purse and collapsed onto the bench next to the door. "Could you pay this kind man, please?"

The driver doffed his hat and backed out the door, fingering the coins the housekeeper gave him. "Thank ye, ma'am. You take care now and call for Speedy Sam anytime. Good day, ladies."

Molly immediately started fussing over Chloe. *If she knew me at all, she'd know how much I despise being mollycoddled. I wish Auntie Clare were here.* She put her hands up to ward off the woman. "I take it Tyler's not home yet so I'm going to bed."

"I'll bring your supper up right away."

"Molly, I know you mean well, but I just want to rest. I'm not hungry." Chloe couldn't help but see the hurt in the woman's eyes and relented. "I would like a cup of tea, though."

"Yes, ma'am. I'll bring it right up."

Chloe had never felt so utterly spent before. The tall four-poster bed looked inviting as she entered the bedroom. She took the time to undress and slipped into a nightgown, then climbed into the welcoming oasis. She barely stirred when Molly tapped on the door and brought in a tray with her tea.

❧❧

"Chloe, you need to wake up. Come on, that a girl." Andrew's face came into focus. Chloe rubbed a hand across her eyes and blinked. "What are you doing in my bedroom, Andrew?" Confused, she searched the room. Only Molly stood by the door. "Where's Tyler?"

Andrew motioned Molly forward. "Molly's going to help you get dressed then I'm taking you to the hospital."

"But Andrew, I'm fine, really."

"It's Tyler. He's been shot. The doctors need to do surgery."

Chloe shook off the cobwebs of sleep and swung her legs over the side of the bed. "Molly, get my clothes. Andrew, get out so I can get dressed." Her legs shook as she shooed him out of the room. The tremors spread up her body, threatening to topple her over. *It can't be! Dear God, not again!*

Now she was thankful for Molly's assistance. Her own fingers trembled so much she could not have buttoned her own dress if she tried. Tears threatened to blind her. "Could you help me down the stairs, please?"

Andrew was pacing the floor like a lumbering bear. The minute he spied Chloe coming down the stairs, he gathered up her coat and waited for her to slip her arms in the sleeves. "I have a carriage waiting. They've taken him to Presbyterian Hospital, supposed to have better surgeons there."

Once they settled in the carriage, she asked the question she was dreading. "How bad is it?"

"The bullet is close to his heart. I know you want it straight. It's not good."

"Andrew, what happened? He was just going to canvas the neighborhood where they found me." A new thought chilled her. "What about Henry?"

Andrew covered her hands with his big paw. "I don't know anything about the boy. He wasn't mentioned. I don't know the particulars—just that Tyler thought you'd been kidnapped again and was being held down on the waterfront by some gang."

Chloe blanched. "He was shot because of me? Because he thought I was in danger?"

Andrew's voice took on a steely quality. "You left the house without telling me, so when Tyler called, I had to tell him you were gone. We both assumed the worst." He leaned in. "Where were you?"

The events of earlier fluttered through her mind. "I was going back to get more pictures to replace the film they destroyed. When I got dizzy and sick to my stomach, I got off the tram and sat in a cafe for a while. Once the nausea and dizziness subsided, I decided to walk and get some fresh air, then I found myself across from Schwarz's Toy Bazaar on Twenty-Third Street. I remembered going to one of Mr. Schwarz's store as a child and since I was feeling better, I decided to explore. "I got hungry so after that I stopped in a little Italian place for some supper. The proprietor, Guido Marcelli, struck up a conversation and before I knew it, I was meeting his whole family and hearing all about how they came to America. I guess I lost track of time." Chloe could see that Andrew's face looked grim and angry even in the relative dark of the coach's interior. "You're furious with me, aren't you?"

"Yes. You had no business sneaking out. I had a job to do and you choose to negate it and me. Now Tyler's paying the price."

Chloe settled back into the upholstery. "I can't tell you how sorry I am—for thwarting you when you were just trying to do your job, but you must know I'd never intentionally set out to hurt my husband."

The carriage pulled to a stop in front of the hospital's main entrance. Andrew got out and extended a hand to Chloe. "I just hope for your sake, he understands that."

Together, they hurried into the lobby. A nurse directed them to the surgical floor waiting room. It was ten minutes of six in the morning before the doctors came out with news.

Anxious, everyone stood. Uncle Teedie, who'd come in the wee hours of the morning, supported Chloe's elbow. Andrew stood on the other side. Superintendent Devery had strode in an hour earlier and stationed men along the corridors after admonishing Roosevelt about security.

The two doctors looked harried. Chloe searched their faces for a hint as to Tyler's condition. They appeared stoic, but not worried. Her heart did a cautious leap. "Doctor?"

The man gave a guarded smile. "Mrs. Reynolds, I presume." He turned to shake Uncle Teedie's hand. "Governor Roosevelt, I'm Doctor Hastings, and this is my colleague Doctor Bennett. Congratulations on the election, sir."

Chloe interrupted. "Doctor, how is my husband?"

He turned back to her and gathered her hands in his own. "He's one strong man. It's a miracle he's alive. That bullet came within mere millimeters of his heart." A smile finally lit up the man's face. "I'm happy to report he made it through surgery and is in recovery at the moment. Don't misunderstand me, he still has a long road ahead." He glanced over at the other doctor. "Doctor Bennett and I are both optimistic Mr. Reynolds will make a full recovery."

Chloe closed her eyes and released the breath she felt like she'd been holding for hours. *Thank you, Jesus.* She smiled up at the surgeon. "When can I see him?" Chloe realized she was crushing the man's fingers and let go.

"You should be able to go up in about thirty minutes, but only long enough to satisfy yourself that he's alive." He gave a short bow. "Now, if you excuse us, Dr. Bennett and I need to get back up there."

Chloe collapsed against the governor's chest. Roosevelt wrapped a fatherly arm around her and patted her shoulder. "There now, sweetheart. God has seen him through the crisis. We need to muster up the courage to see him through his recovery."

"I just hope he'll forgive me."

"In my book, forgiveness is part and parcel in marriage and love. There isn't any mistaking Tyler loves you. Your job will be to help him remember that."

Chloe reached up and kissed his cheek. "Thank you, Uncle Teedie."

The afternoon sun was slanting through the window before Tyler stirred. Chloe jumped up from her perch at the side of his bed. "Tyler, darling, I'm here. Can you open your eyes?"

His dark lashes fluttered against his pale skin and then slowly opened. He licked his lips. "Water," he whispered.

Chloe filled a glass halfway and stabbed a paper straw into it. "Andrew, can you lift his head?" She held the glass while Tyler took a few sips.

The effort seemed to exhaust him. Chloe thought he'd gone back to sleep when he spoke again. "What happened?"

Andrew gave Chloe a challenging look. "You want me to tell him? I got the whole story from Superintendent Devery when he showed up."

Chloe stood by the window while Andrew shared the details that led up to the shooting. Afraid to see the accusation in her husband's eyes, she listened to the story with her back turned. *Andrew's right. It really is all my fault.* Now two men are dead and the man she loved was fighting for his own life.

Would he blame her? Last time Tyler had been shot, he accused her of trying to kill him. It was only a spilled bowl of hot soup, but the anger behind his words hurt. She thought she'd gotten over the pain his words inflicted. Now she wasn't so sure. What if he took his angry out on her again? She ran away last time. *God help me, I'll not run this time.*

❧❧

113

Tyler took in everything Andrew was saying. He remembered the details of the stakeout and what led up to it, but learning Chloe hadn't been kidnapped brought on a mix of emotions. Relieved she was okay. At the same time, he couldn't help being upset with her for putting herself into potential danger without thinking of the consequences. He looked over to where she stood; the sun outlining the beautiful contours of her face. He wanted to throttle her and yet wrap her in his arms at the same time. Love overcame the angry.

"Andrew, could you give us a few minutes?" Tyler waited until his friend left the room. "Chloe? Darling, come here."

She turned and looked at him. It speared his heart to see the fear in her eyes. She didn't move except to wipe away a tear that trailed down her cheek. "You have every right to be angry with me. I wasn't thinking. All I knew was I needed to get more pictures." She dropped her chin to her chest and worried the hankie in her hand. "And now men have lost their lives, and you were almost killed. It was stupid. I was stupid."

Tyler's heart wrenched. "I said come here." She didn't move. "Please?"

Chloe stepped hesitantly up to the bed. Tyler could see the exhaustion in her red-rimmed eyes and the sag of her shoulders. She still looked ill. Her normally smooth complexion was blotchy. Her black hair was missing the silky sheen he couldn't get enough of. Any anger he harbored vanished in a wave of concern. He reached for her hand. A sharp stab of pain made him grimace.

Chloe gasped and leaned in. "Are you okay? Do you want me to call a nurse?"

Tyler gave himself a moment to let the pain ease. He opened his eyes to see her looking down at him in alarm. "I'm fine, or I will be if you'll be my nurse. As I recall you were pretty good at it." He smiled to reassure her he was okay.

Her face twisted. Her lips trembled, and a fresh wave of tears gushed. "Oh, Tyler, I'm so, so sorry. I never meant for any of this to happen. Will you ever be able to forgive me?"

"Okay."

Chloe was confused. "Okay? What do you mean 'okay'?"

"Okay, I'll forgive you, but just so you know, I would have been down on that dock, regardless. You weren't going to be safe until those lowlifes were caught." He opened his hand and wiggled his fingers. She wove her own between his. Relief overwhelmed her.

"But, wife of mine," he took on a serious tone, "the next time you decided to defy my husbandly orders, I may just have to turn you over my knee."

Chloe gave a dramatic gasp. "You wouldn't!"

"Try me." Tyler hesitated. "On second thought, don't try me. I don't want to go through this again."

Chloe laid her bandaged hand alongside his face and leaned in close. "Oh, Tyler, I was scared to death I was going to lose you. Promise me you won't put yourself in harm's way again."

He searched her face and looked away. "I don't make promises I can't keep. That way no one is disappointed."

Chloe didn't think he was talking about her and him anymore. "You've never broken a promise to me, so who are you talking about?"

With his head still turned, he whispered. "My sisters."

Chloe kept a hold of his hand and lowered herself to the chair next to his bed. "I remember you said you had two sisters who died."

Tyler looked up at the ceiling and let out a deep sigh. "Pamela and Myrna. They were nine and seven. I was twelve. My Pa got sick too, but the girls were real bad. Ma sent me for the doctor. He was tending a dozen other people, mostly kids, who'd taken ill. It was cholera. By the time I got back with the doc, Pammy and Myrnie were gone." He closed his eyes. Chloe could see the muscle work along his jaw. "I promised them I'd save them. I didn't."

Chloe's heart ached for him. She knew what it was like not to be able to save someone you love, no matter if you could have done anything or not. She got up and put her hands on either side of his face. "Look at me, please. I love you, Tyler Joseph Reynolds, but you're not God. You can't keep trying to make up for something you had no control over."

Tyler gave her a weak smile. "I seem to lose the people I love. I don't want to lose you too."

Chloe could see the anguish in his eyes. "You're a good man and a good husband, that's enough for me."

CHAPTER 23

Chloe stood dressed and ready to go when Andrew knocked on her bedroom door. "Coming." She looked and felt better this morning. She would have stayed at the hospital had the doctors let her. Now she was glad for a good night's sleep in her own bed. She gave her reflection one last inspection, pleased to see the dark circles under her eyes had faded and there was color in her cheeks.

Andrew didn't look half as good. His face was haggard and showed the dark shadow of unshaven beard.

"Didn't you sleep well?"

Andrew stretched like a bear coming out of hibernation and rubbed a fist down the small of his back. "That bed might be good for a kid like Henry, but it's a mite short and soft for a guy like me."

Chloe gasped and brought her hands up to her mouth. "Oh, my goodness, with everything that's happened, I've forgotten all about Henry! Where is he? He wasn't with Tyler at the docks was he?"

Andrew scratched his head. "I figured you two sent him on back to the district. Was kinda surprised after Christmas and everything. I reckoned you decided you weren't ready to be instant parents."

Chloe rushed to the stairs. "I have to go get him. That poor child must think we abandoned him."

Andrew stomped down the steps two at a time, reaching the bottom before Chloe. "Whoa, hold on there. Tyler would have my hide if I let you go back down there. That Morello fella and half his gang are still on the loose. I'll bet you a pound to a penny they still have an interest in you, especially after the coppers snagged all that counterfeit money." He pulled on his coat. "Tell you what, I'll drop you off at the hospital so I know you're safe, then I'll go hunt down Henry. What do you want me to do with him when I find him?"

Chloe worked her arms into her coat sleeves. "Gather all his belongs—there can't be much from what Tyler described—and bring him to the hospital. We really haven't talked about it, but I think Tyler expects for us to provide that child a home and I intend to make sure that happens."

❧❧

As soon as Andrew handed her off to the police officer guarding Tyler's room, he had the hired hack take him to the Lower Eastside. He cursed the morning traffic of buggies, wagons, and pedestrians that clogged the narrow streets. This poor, working-class neighborhood was not where Andrew expected to find himself on this cold, wintery morning.

The carriage swayed with his weight as he stepped down. "Wait here for me." He surveyed the intersection and spied a young newsboy hawking papers.

"Get your paper here," the kid shouted. "Gangsters killed, counterfeit money confiscated."

"Hey you, kid, you know a newsie named Henry Perkins?"

The boy stepped back. His eyes traveled all the way up Andrew's large frame until they landed on his face. "Golly, mister, you're as big as the statue of that lady holding the torch out in the harbor."

Andrew squatted down on his haunches to be closer to eye level with the tow-headed kid. "I come from a land of giants. Ever heard of Jack and the Beanstalk?" The boy nodded, mouth agape. "That was my brother. Now, tell me, you know a kid goes by the moniker Two Bits?"

The boy swallowed. "Hank has the corner a block over on Fourteenth. You ain't gonna eat him, are you?"

"Not today, I already had my breakfast." Andrew laughed and flipped the boy a nickel. Two blocks over, he spied Henry standing on the street corner wearing his old clothes. The kid was doing a brisk business, if the small pile of papers under his arm was any indication. Andrew had the driver pull up next to the curb. "Hey Hank, where are your new duds?"

Henry squinted one eye and gave Andrew a scowl. "What you doin' here? Slummin'?"

Andrew could see the kid was upset. He pointed to the paper Hank brought up to shield his face from the bright sunlight. "You know that shooting down on the docks. Tyler was there. Got himself shot pretty bad. That's why he didn't come back and get you."

Henry's whole countenance changed. The tough guy act disappeared as he ran up to the carriage. "He ain't dead is he? The paper didn't say nuttin' about a detective gettin' shot."

"Nah, he's too ornery to die. Miss Chloe sent me to fetch you. I'm supposed to take you to the hospital."

"Just a sec." The kid raced across the street, dodging horses and wagons. Andrew watched him hand his pile of papers off to another boy and run back. "Let's go. I want to see Mr. Tyler."

"First, we need to get all your stuff."

Henry scrunched up his nose and gave Andrew a puzzled look. "How come?"

"Seems you, young man, have a new home. That is, if you want one."

He looked skeptical. "You're not joshin' me, are ya? That's would be a pretty low kinda thing to do to a kid."

Andrew laughed. "Nope. Honest Injun." A grin broke out on the kid's face and he let out a 'wahoo'!

❧❧

Tyler watched Chloe closely to see if he could tell she really meant what she was saying. "So you truly want Hank to come live with us on a permanent basis?"

"Yes. He needs a home, and I saw how quickly you two bonded." Chloe laughed. "It was like watching three little boys with you, Andrew, and Henry wrestling around the Christmas tree." She cocked her head to one side. "You weren't planning on taking him back to that hovel you described, were you?"

In truth, Tyler hadn't given it much more thought since that day on the stairs at the house. "I meant to talk to you about that. Guess I've kind of had other things on my mind, like your safety. But, you're right, that boy needs a home and I think we can provide a pretty good one once I'm up and around again. Truthfully, I already asked him."

Chloe raised her eyebrows. Before they could discuss it any farther, Andrew knocked on the open door. "You ready for a bit of company, Sherlock?"

Henry stood, hat in hand beside him, and chewed his bottom lip.

Chloe slid down from her perch on the side of Tyler's bed and held her arms open. "Henry, I'm so glad you're here." The boy hesitated, then allowed himself to be folded into her embrace. Confusion and embarrassment covered his face. As tiny as Chloe was, she still stood taller than Hank, but not by much.

He looked up at her. "Mister Andrew said you want me to live with you. You sure you don't want a baby or maybe a puppy instead of me?" He wiggled out of her arms and crossed them. "I'm thirteen... well, almost thirteen. I ain't no prize, ya know."

Tyler chuckled and grimaced. He would have to remember not to do that for a while. "Hank, we aren't looking for a prize, we're looking for a son, and I think you fit the bill just fine. Right, Chloe?"

She reached out as if to hug him again. The boy backed up a step. She let her arms drop and tried a smile Tyler thought was genuine. "I've never been around boys much, so you'll have to let me know when I get to mushy and I can be a little bossy." Tyler snorted. She gave him a look. "But I think I'd really like having a chance to be your mother if you'll let me."

Tyler could see the struggle going on in the kid. Hank had fended for himself a long time and answered to no one. He remembered how he'd yearned to run off and be a cowboy when he was the boy's age, especially after his sisters died and his mother seemed to smother him with undeserved attention. "Well, what do you think?"

Hank remained quiet, scuffing the toe of his worn out boot against the floor. When Chloe started to reach a hand out, Tyler cleared his throat to warn her. They needed to give the kid some space to work through everything in his head.

"Just so you know, there'll be rules and you'll be expected to go to school, do chores, and respect us as your parents. It will also mean you'll have a family that will stand behind you a hundred percent, no matter what." Tyler rested his head back against the pillow and waited. The room filled with a heavy stillness. An ache, unrelated to his injuries, moved across his heart. He hadn't realized how much this meant to him. The boy's silence hurt. "Andy, maybe you'd better take Hank back."

Henry's head jerked up. "No! I mean I want to stay with you." He leaned in and clutched the metal footboard. "I'll be a real good son, I promise. I'll do everything you ask without no fussin', it's just that..."

When he didn't finish, Chloe stepped up and laid a hand on the boy's shoulder. "Just what? You know whatever you tell us won't make a difference how we feel about you."

Hank searched her face and turned to Tyler. "Don't you remember, I ain't had no proper schoolin'. People—let that fancy man in the top hat wearin' the eye piece on a string—they're not gonna be too keen on you takin' the likes of me in and calling me your son."

"Uncle Teedie? He'd be the first to welcome you with open arms." Chloe jutted out her chin. "Anyone else with that kind of an attitude doesn't deserve to be called a friend and I don't care what strangers might say. As for school, Mr. Tyler's right, you'll have to attend school, but maybe you and I could work together and get you caught up with the kids your age so they won't know any difference."

Atta girl. Tyler couldn't have been prouder of her. Hank would be lucky to have a mother like her—as lucky as he was to have her for his wife.

CHAPTER 24

New Year's Eve proved to be a quiet affair. Tyler was home from the hospital and under doctor's orders to remain inside, preferably in bed. That lasted about two hours, then Chloe gave up and allowed him to join her and Henry in the parlor. They spend the evening alternating between listening to Henry read to them from his favorite Sherlock Holmes story and Tyler teaching him how to play chess. Although he tired quickly, he seemed to be recovering much faster this time compared to the last time he was shot.

"I have an idea." Chloe jumped up. "I know a perfect way to try out my new camera. I'll be right back." She hurried from the room to retrieve the Christmas present Tyler had so thoughtfully given her and a comb for Henry's hair. She came back to find Tyler trying to work his arms into his jacket, grim determination on his face. "Oh, let me help you with that."

Henry tucked in his shirt. "Why do we have to get all gussied up? You ain't gonna make me go to church again, are ya?"

"No, we're *not* going to church. Now stand still and let me comb your hair." He scowled but submitted. "I think we should have a family picture. Let me just get my tripod set up. The bulb attachment should be long enough for me to reach."

Henry helped her pull her father's chair around and had Tyler set in it with Henry standing to his side. "Good, now I'll stand on this side." The rubber tube wasn't quite long enough. "My arms are too short. Tyler, trade me places." He stood with effort. "No, that won't work, you're too tall. I'll bring the camera closer."

She perched on the arm of the chair and rested one hand on his shoulder. Henry followed her example and straddled a leg over the arm on the other side. He leaned in to rest his elbow on Tyler's shoulder. It wasn't the classic pose most photographers used, which suited Chloe just fine. "Now, smile!"

❦

The next morning, Chloe sat down with Henry to see exactly where he stood academically. The boy surprised her. He already demonstrated how well he could read, and she found his mathematic skills were excellent as well. "Where did you learn to work figures?"

Henry shrugged. "I had to know how to make change so people wouldn't cheat me."

"I supposed you learned to read from the newspapers you sold."

"My ma taught me my letters. I just figured out the rest myself. It was pretty easy."

Chloe stood and gathered the books and papers from the table. "Well, young man, I'm pleased to inform you, you are definitely ready for school. When it goes back into session next week, we'll go down and get you enrolled in the seventh grade. How about you and I explored the neighborhood taking pictures while Tyler rests?"

Bundled up against the cold, they search out interesting things to photograph. Henry surprised her with his attention to small details and patterns. *He certainly has an artist's eye.* They found a nice park two blocks down where a couple of boys were playing. They invited Henry to join them.

He turned to her, hope written all over his face. "Can I?"

"It's may I, and yes you may. I'm going home to check on Tyler. Be back in time for lunch."

Henry grinned from ear to ear and raced off. "Yes, ma'am!"

They spent the evening listening to Henry regale them with stories of his new best friends, Jimmy and Noah Lansing. Seeing the pinched look of desperation gone from his young face made Chloe's heart happy. She snuggled next to Tyler. "I'm glad he's here, aren't you?" When he didn't answer, she turned and looked up at her husband. He was staring into the fire, lost in thought. "Tyler, darling, what is it?"

He tore his gaze away from the flames and smiled down at her. "Nothing really. It's just that today TR stepped down as Governor. As his aide, I should have been there. We had a whole agenda of things he wanted to get accomplished this past week before he turned over power to Ben Odell."

Chloe laid her head on his chest. "I'm sure Uncle Teedie understands. It wasn't like you got shot and were in the hospital on purpose."

He squeezed her shoulder. "There's also the fact that we'll miss the trip to Colorado. I know how much you were looking forward to seeing Clare and Abel, not to mention the trip up to Brown's Park we had planned while TR was hunting."

"We'll go another time when you well and healthy. Besides, that will give me time to get over whatever this malady is. Right now I don't think I'm up to the long train ride either."

❧❧

By mid-January, New York City was digging out from back-to-back snowstorms. Although still in the low teens, the day broke bright and clear. Chloe settled into the rocking chair Clare had kept in the corner of the kitchen the whole time Chloe was growing up. It now set next to the window in a cozy corner of the parlor in the brownstone. The bouts of nausea and dizziness hadn't subsided, leaving her exhausted. She looked down at her hand. Tiny dots along a seam in her palm were the only reminder of her ordeal with the counterfeiters.

Working her finger, she played with her wedding ring. It was a simple gold band with a small topaz stone and baguette diamonds on either side. It fit the size of her hand much better than the ostentatious engagement ring Lucius had given her. The ring had disappeared, along with Lucius. His escape from the courthouse having been successful, no one had seen him since. Chloe leaned her head back. After all he had done, she still couldn't hate the man. "I hope you find your way."

"I ain't lost." Henry scurried across the room, heading to the kitchen.

"I'm *not* lost."

Henry stopped and scratched his head. "If you ain't lost and I ain't lost, who are you talkin' to?"

Chloe chuckled. "Neither one of us is lost. We are both very much found. I was thinking of someone I used to know. I was also correcting your grammar. Ain't is *not* a word. You need to figure out a better word to replace it when you speak."

"Yes, ma'am. Can I have another muffin? I'm pretty sure one won't last until lunchtime."

"Yes, you may, and take two to Jimmy and Noah. They probably have holes in their stomachs the same place you do."

Henry laughed. "Probably. Since the school is still closed until they get the roof fixed we're gonna work on our fort. Mrs. Lansing said we could eat our lunch out there." He started to push the swinging door open. "You and Mr. Tyler will be back before supper, right?"

Chloe could read the insecurity in the boy's voice. He still didn't know if he could trust them not to leave him. If Tyler hadn't demanded she get a full physical exam, they wouldn't be going back to Philly, and when Doctor Moore heard what had been going on, he agreed. She chalked it up to fatigue, but Tyler wouldn't let it drop, so they were making the trip back to Philadelphia to see the elderly physician that had delivered Chloe and been at her mother's bedside when she died.

"Yes, we're taking the afternoon train back from Philadelphia. Remember, you can always call Andrew if there's a problem. Jimmy and Noah's mother knows you're staying the whole day. Are you sure you don't want to come along?"

"Nah, I don't like doctors, besides Jimmy and Noah need my help. Neither one of them can build a strong snow wall worth beans. See ya." He waved and disappeared through the door.

CHAPTER 25

Chloe buttoned her blouse and sat down to lace up her boots. "Well, doctor? What's the verdict? Do I have some exotic disease or just the everyday malady most women face?"

The doctor pushed his spectacles back up the rise of his hawk-shaped nose and smiled. "I believe I've come to an accurate diagnosis. We should include your husband in on this."

He went to the door and ushered Tyler into the room. Worry etched his handsome face as he settled into a chair next to Chloe. Dr. Moore moved behind his desk. His neutral expression gave nothing away. He looked up at the couple and smiled. "It is my expert opinion that you, my lovely lady, are about three months pregnant. Congratulations! I hope this is happy news."

Chloe's mouth fell open. She couldn't seem to shut it on her own accord. A wild wash of emotions flooded through her. She'd been disappointed when she didn't become pregnant right away. Every month for the past six months, she felt the frustrating letdown of having her menses start. Now that she thought back on it, the last few months they'd been so light as to be nonexistent.

Tyler interrupted her thoughts and pulled her back into the moment. "You're telling me my wife is going to have a baby?" He stood up and ran his hands through his hair, sending it into curly, dark copper waves on his head.

Doctor Moore laughed. "That's exactly what I'm telling you. If my calculations are correct, your little bundle of joy should arrive sometime in late July. Of course, we'll be more certain as we go along."

Chloe still sat, the idea of a baby taking full form in her mind. *A baby! I'm going to have a baby!*

Tyler pulled her to her feet and crushed her to him then as abruptly pushed her away. "Oh, my gosh, I didn't hurt you, did I? Here, sit down." He gently lowered her back into the chair.

Chloe laughed and laid a hand across her flat stomach. "Silly man, you can't hurt a baby by hugging his mama."

Tyler turned back to the doctor. "Is she going to be okay? Is there anything we—I need to do?"

Doctor Moore chuckled. "Just enjoy this time. I recommend getting Kellogg's book 'Ladies Guide in Health & Disease'. I agree with Kellogg—a good healthy diet and moderate exercise are key to a healthy pregnancy."

"Can I continue working?" Chloe asked.

Tyler gave her an incredulous look. "How can you even ask that after what you've been through?" He crossed his arms and shook his head. "I forbid it. You cannot take a chance and put yourself and our baby in danger again."

Chloe's temper rose instantly. How dare he! She stood and crossed her own arms. "You may be my husband, but this is 1901. Women have rights, you know. Lots of women work while they're pregnant." She turned to the doctor for support. "Tell him, doctor."

Doctor Moore rubbed a hand across the back of his neck. "Well, you're not working in a factory for twelve hours a day so you should be fine."

Tyler started to interrupt.

The doctor held up a hand to stop him. "But, you definitely can't be traipsing around New York's more unsavory boroughs in your condition. The trauma you experienced could easily have ended this pregnancy. I would suggest you move back to Philadelphia where Mrs. Morrison can keep an eye on you."

Chloe sighed at the mention of Clare. "She's not in Philly anymore. Her and Abel moved to Colorado. Besides, we'll be moving to Washington DC." A new worry surfaced at the mention of DC. "Doctor Moore, I'll be okay to travel, right? I want you to deliver our baby."

He turned from Chloe to Tyler. "You know I delivered this little lady, came out kicking and screaming as I recall." He chuckled and gathered Chloe's hand in his own. "I'd be honored to help bring your son or daughter into this world. You do realize Washington is a ways away and babies are notorious for not arriving when expected?

"I think it would be wise to have a doctor close by. I can give you the names of a few I highly recommend. Until then, I'd be glad to see you if you would feel more comfortable. As far as traveling goes, this is a new century. Women aren't confined to hide away from society during pregnancy. You should be safe to travel until mid-June if the remainder of your pregnancy is uneventful."

❧❧

Tyler shook the doctor's hand. "Thank you, sir. As Chloe said, we're moving to Washington the first part of March. I'll be sure she comes in before then." He ushered Chloe from the room, his feet barely touching the floor. *A baby! I'm going to be a father!*

Chloe seemed unusually quiet as he helped her into the coach. He climbed in beside her and wrapped an arm around her. "Can you imagine, we're going to be parents? I mean we already are to Hank, but this is different."

Chloe laid her head on his chest and sniffed.

Tyler turned in the seat and lifted her chin so he could look into her eyes. She blinked, releasing a tear to trail down her cheek. Her eyes reflected her misery.

Fear and worry grabbed him by the throat. "Chloe, darling, what's wrong? I imagined you'd be happy about this."

She dashed a shaky finger under her eye. "I am, honestly. It's the most wonderful news. It's just that…" An anguished sob broke loose. "I don't know how to be a mother."

Relief washed the tension from Tyler's body. He'd worried she was unhappy about the baby. He stifled a laugh; sure she would not appreciate it if she thought he was dismissing her qualms. Instead, he placed a gentle kiss on her forehead. "I've watched you with Hank, you're a natural. I have absolutely no doubt you'll be an amazing mama to our baby."

Her dark eyes searched his. "Henry's different. He's half grown. I don't know anything about babies." She chewed on her lip. "I wish Auntie Clare were here. I'd feel so much better."

During the train ride back to New York City, a constant flow of thoughts tumbled through Tyler's brain. He was going to have not one child, but two to support. Now he didn't see how his plan of being a public defender or venturing out on his own to provide legal counsel to the working class and poor was going to work. One scenario after another played out in his mind, and the longer he dwelled on them, the more anxious he got.

◈◈

Chloe was glad Tyler was quiet on the train ride home. She needed time to think. A baby would be sure to change her whole world. What about her budding career? She loved being a journalist and photographer. *How can I give that up?* She knew she'd have no choice. With Clare and Abel gone, they were on their own. If Tyler quit working for Uncle Teedie, they would never be able to afford any live-in help. *There's sure to be more babies. I'm going to be just like all those poor women I've been defending—so worn out caring for a family I'll lose my own identity.* Panic began to rise.

CHAPTER 26

It was Tyler's first day back to a full schedule working out of the temporary office Uncle Teedie had arranged so Mr. Odell could step into his new position as governor of New York. Chloe leaned against the front door and sighed, happy her husband had mended and was healthy again. As much as she loved him, it would be nice not having him under foot anymore. The longer he was forced to be inactive, the grouchier he got.

With Henry off to school, Tyler otherwise occupied, and a blessed reprieve from morning sickness, Chloe hoped to get a few things done between the bouts of fatigue she was still experiencing. She made a mental list as she climbed the stairs. *I have five weeks to us get ready to move to DC.*

She opened the wardrobe in the extra bedroom and sighed. It was crammed with old clothes she'd never wear again. Images of the women and children she had seen in the sewing room of the old tenement flashed across her mind. "I'll box these up and take them down to the district."

Pleased with her idea, she began sorting and folding things into boxes. Making progress, she turned to grab the next item. She ran her hand over the wool tweed, now dirty and missing several buttons. It was the old coat she'd worn down in the garment district so as not to be conspicuous. "I won't need this anymore." She sighed and contemplated the exposé she wanted to do about the illegal use of child labor.

Pressing the folded coat into a box, she felt a small bulge along the hem. "What in the world?" Putting her hand down inside the pocket, she found a hole in the lining and worked her fingers through to retrieve a small cylinder. "Oh, my goodness!" It was the first roll of film she'd taken the day she was tied up and left by the thugs running the counterfeiting scam and illegal sweatshop.

Excitement course through her at what she might find on the film. "Tyler darling, look what I found." Chloe rushed into the master bedroom and stopped short, forgetting he wasn't there. "Oh, pooh." She wrestled with waiting until he came home to go down to DeYoung's studio to develop the film. She'd promised not to go back to the garment district, but the studio was blocks away from there.

Chloe looked at the clock on the dresser and chewed her lip. *Three o'clock. If I go now, I could be back with the actual pictures before he even knows I'm gone.* Her mind made up, she reached into her desk drawer and pulled out a small travel case of paper. She'd leave him a note just in case he left early and beat her home. Putting away her writing case, she noticed the corner of an envelope sticking out of the jumble in her drawer. It was the letter her father had left for her to give to her brother once she found him. A picture of Sundance standing next to the corral at the Bassett ranch filled her mind. Where was he? Was he safe? Was he still alive?

Even though he denied it, Chloe was sure the man everyone knew as Sundance Kid was her brother. There was too much evidence to convince her otherwise. Now, handling the envelope, she felt bad for not thinking more about him. Thoughts of Harry Longabaugh had been overshadowed by the upheaval happening in her life, which was the way he'd wanted it.

She ran a finger over her father's familiar handwriting. She hated the fact that she'd failed to fulfill his last wish. "Sorry, Papa." With a sigh, she laid it back in the case and latched it. She was just about to close the drawer when something prompted her to pull the envelope back out. With the film in one hand and the letter in the other, she headed down the stairs in search of Henry.

The kitchen was empty. Cookie crumbs and an empty glass gave evidence that he'd been there. She checked the other rooms. The boy was nowhere to be found. Chloe pulled on her coat, hat, and gloves. "He's probably at the park with the Lansing boys. I believe it's time for a lesson in asking permission."

She walked the two blocks to the park and scanned the area. There were a couple dozen kids scampering around in the new fallen snow. With no hills close by, they were taking turns pulling each other on toboggans and sleds.

Spying Henry's red trapper hat bobbing up and down behind a wall of snow, she picked her way across the open space. "Henry." She waved to get his attention as he launched another snowball at the opposing team.

He stood up and yelled, "Time out." He trotted over to where she stood and wiped a gloved hand across his red nose. "Yes, ma'am?"

Chloe pulled a hankie from her pocket. "Here, use this. I'm glad I found you. Do you realize I didn't know where you were?"

Henry shrugged his shoulders and glanced back at the snowball fight that had commenced without him. "Didn't think about it." He cocked his head and squinted one eye up at her. "Do I have to ask every time I want to go someplace?"

Chloe thought about how much it rankled her to have to ask permission or be told she couldn't do something. "Listen, I understand you haven't had anyone to answer to for a long time but Mr. Tyler and I need to know where you are so we don't worry needlessly."

Henry scrunched up his face. "Why would you worry? I know how to take care of myself."

Chloe chuckled. "Believe me, I tell Mr. Tyler that all the time." She thought for a moment, tapping her finger against her chin. "I think it's more about common courtesy in a family. When people care about each other, they want to know they're safe."

Henry pushed out his bottom lip and nodded his head in understanding. "Sounds okay. I'll try and remember next time. It's okay if I stay, isn't it? We're winning and I have the best aim."

"Sure. I have to go out for a while. I left a note for Mr. Tyler in case he gets home before I return. I expect you home before it gets dark, okay?"

"Okay." Henry took off back across the snow-covered ground.

"Hey, Henry," Chloe called out. When he stopped and turned, she lobbed the snowball she'd quickly formed. It hit him square in the chest and explored.

"Nice shot. Next time you can be on my team." He waved and ran off to join his friends.

❧

The trolley took her almost to the doorstep of DeYoung's Studio at Union Square on Broadway. She'd met Joseph DeYoung at a social function and their shared interested in photography had blossomed into a professional friendship. When he had made the trip to Philadelphia to take their wedding portrait, he offered her the use of his developing room whenever she needed it. She looked forward to seeing him again as she stepped into the warm interior, to the tinkling of a bell over the door.

"I'll be right with you," came a man's voice from behind a red velvet curtain. DeYoung stepped out wiping his hands on a rag. "Ah, Chloe Reynolds, so good to see you again. What brings you to my humble studio?"

Chloe removed her glove and extended her hand to the pleasant looking man. He was in his late twenties with longish, mouse brown hair and side-whiskers. His smile matched his friendly eyes. "Mr. DeYoung, I was hoping to use of your darkroom."

"Certainly. Right this way and its Joseph, not Mr. DeYoung." He led her back through the curtain to his darkroom. "Do you have more of those glorious landscapes? I still think you should let me set up a showing."

"No, this roll is… was for an article I was working on." Chloe took in the neat and organized room. *I'd like a darkroom like this someday.* She had done her own developing while in college with a dozen other students sharing the same space. To say it was cramped and cluttered to the point of being dysfunctional, was putting it mildly.

The faint tinkling of the bell drew Joseph's attention away from the stack of collodion paper he'd moved down to be in easy reach for her. "Hopefully that's a paying customer. I'll be up front if you need me."

He disappeared and Chloe went to work. The process was magical for her as she watched the images she'd captured materialize before her eyes. "These are good, really good, even if I do say so myself."

Joseph didn't return, so she finished up and left the prints to dry. Making her way to the front, she passed the opening where he had his camera equipment set up. Curious, Chloe stopped and glanced in. A man stood with his back to her, counting out money into Joseph's hand. She must have made a sound because the tall stranger turned to look at her.

She gasped and brought her hand to her throat. "Sundance!"

Shock crossed his face. He collected himself, said something to Joseph, and came to her. "Chloe, what are you doing here?" He looked back. Joseph ducked his head and began counting out the bills in his hand. Sundance grabbed her elbow and steered her out of the room.

"I can't believe it's you." She wanted to hug him. "What are you doing in New York? Have you given up robbing trains and banks?"

Sundance held up his hands. "First of all, please don't call me Sundance. Mr. DeYoung and the rest of New York thinks I'm Harry Place." He smiled down at her and studied her face. "You look different, almost radiant. Marriage must agree with you."

"Why, thank you."

"I have to say I was upset when I first heard Trace Rawlings was really a Pinkerton agent and that you'd married him. If I remember right, there were a lot of sparks flying between you two."

Chloe blushed and laughed. "There still are. We're expecting our first child." She laid a hand over her stomach, even though the rounding of her belly didn't show through her heavy coat.

Harry fingered his derby. "I'm happy for you. Trace, I mean Tyler, is a good man even if he was out to get me." He glanced out the front window. "I have someone I'd like you to meet."

"I'll be back in a minute," she called to the photographer as Sundance pulled her out the front door and onto the sidewalk where a pretty woman waited.

"Ethel, this is my… this is Chloe, the friend from Pennsylvania I told you about."

He talked about me? Hope stirred in her soul. Chloe shook hands with the woman, who was the spitting image of Ann Bassett. "Please to meet you." She looked back at Sundance. "She looks more like Ann's sister than Josie."

He laughed. "I know." He wrapped an arm around the woman's waist. "Ethel and I are leaving the country. Butch is going with us." A shadow of regret crossed his face. "I'm tired of looking over my shoulder. So is he."

"But, you can't leave, I just found you again." Chloe tried to keep the pleading tone out of her voice and failed.

"Nothing's changed." He gave her a sad smile.

"When do you leave?" She hated the spoiled, petulant sound in her voice. *So much for sounding like a grown woman.*

"Tomorrow. We sail out on the RMS Herminius for Buenos Aires."

Joseph DeYoung pushed his studio door open and poked his head out. "Mrs. Reynolds, is everything okay?"

Chloe needed more time. "Can we go someplace and talk?" she asked Sundance.

He laid a hand on her arm, his blue eyes expressing his resolve. "There's really nothing to talk about. Ethel and I have to go." He leaned down and brushed her cheek with a kiss. "You have a good life and take care of yourself." He released her and turned away.

Chloe remembered the letter she'd stuffed in her pocket. "Harry, wait!" She pulled the battered envelope out and ran the few steps to where he paused on the sidewalk. "This is for you."

He gave her a quizzical look and shoved it in the inside pocket of his overcoat. "You take care, Chloe girl."

She watched them walk away, arm in arm, and wondered if she'd ever see him again.

CHAPTER 27

Tyler paced the length of the room and back again. "What should I do?"

Back in their temporary New York offices after a month-long hunting trip, Roosevelt shuffled the stack together and put it back in the large envelope. "If you want my opinion, you need to let her finish this."

Tyler lowered himself into a chair across from where TR sat behind a borrowed desk. "What if there are repercussions? Morello's still a strong force in the boroughs. He might want revenge after we closed down their counterfeiting operation and Chloe's name would be on the byline. He could put two and two together and hurt her to get to me."

TR nodded his head and pursed his lips in thought. "The man still has power in New York, much to my chagrin, but my sources assure me his arm doesn't reach as far as Washington." He leaned forward and rested his elbows on the desktop. "We're scheduled to be there in a week. Why don't you two plan on going down as soon as she turns her article in? That way she's out of harm's way and it will give you a few extra days to settle in before the inauguration."

Tyler mulled over TR suggestion. It might prove to be their solution, since Chloe wasn't about to give up the opportunity to finish her exposé. He had to admit her work was good. The pictures alone told a poignant story and the eloquence and feeling she wrote the accompanying article with, were sure to raise an outcry across the country.

"As much as I want to keep her safe, I can't deny her this." His mind made up, he pulled himself out of the chair and reached across to shake TR's hand. "Thank you, sir. I'll see you in Washington."

❦❦

Chloe wrung her hands and lifted the curtain for the hundredth time. *Where is he?* The street remained empty. She turned back to the room and surveyed the sea of boxes. It was definite. She hated moving. She listened to the murmur of little boy voices coming from the stack. Henry and his friends had made themselves a cave among the boxes.

She needed a distraction. "Boys, are you hungry?" It was a stupid question. Henry never passed up a chance to eat. Where he put it all, Chloe wasn't sure. After comparing notes with Bridgette Lansing, she found out Jimmy and Noah were just as bad.

A ruckus erupted, and three heads popped up. "Yes, ma'am."

Henry played spokesman. "A slice of pie would be real good about now."

Chloe chuckled and waded through the brown box sea toward the kitchen. "Nice try. I have some biscuits you can spread a little preserves on. The pie is for dessert tonight. Remember Andrew is coming over." Chloe stopped to rearrange a couple of boxes.

The snack substitute forgotten, Henry pumped a fist in the air and turned back to his friends. "Alright. You guys should see Andrew. He's a bona fide giant. Must be seven feet tall and has to turn sideways to get through the door."

"Is that true, Mrs. Reynolds, or is Hank just pulling our legs?" The oldest Lansing boy asked.

Chloe laughed. "It's true. Now go wash up."

Before Chloe could pull the biscuits out of the warmer, the three boys exploded into the room. "Can Jimmy and Noah stay for supper? Pleeeease…" Henry clasped his hands and gave her his most pleading look.

"Aren't you doing a sleep-over at their house tonight?"

The boys huddled, then came apart. Henry remained the spokesman for the trio. "We can eat here and then go to their house. You could call Mrs. Lansing and let her know. She'd probably enjoy a meal with just Mr. Lansing for a change."

Chloe arched an eyebrow and snorted. "I'm sure she would. It's thoughtful of you three to think of that." She took her time cutting and buttering the biscuits, feeling three sets of eyes watching and ears waiting anxiously for her decision.

"You can take this back to your cave, but first you'd better call your mom, Jimmy, and ask her for permission to stay for supper."

Whoops and hollers followed the boys back out the kitchen door. It swung back and stuck open. Chloe heard Noah say, "your ma's real nice and boy can she cook." Jimmy added, "and pretty too." Henry replied, "Yeah, I'm really lucky to have a ma like her."

Her heart contracted and quick tears filled her eyes. *Ma, he called me ma!*

When Tyler found her back in the rocker an hour later, she was still giddy and teary-eyed. Instant concern clouded his face as he dropped to one knee in front of her and braced a hand on her chair's arms. "Chloe, darling, what's the matter? Are you in pain? Is it the baby?"

Chloe giggled and dashed a loose tear away. "No, I'm fine. In fact, I'm wonderful." She looked into Tyler's eyes. "Come in the kitchen and I'll tell you all about it."

Chloe poured him a cup of coffee. "Henry called me ma today." She joined him with a cup of her own. "Not directly, but that's how he referred to me. I thought it'd take a long time. I was prepared for that. I'm his mama." She couldn't wipe the smile off her face.

Tyler sipped his coffee. "That's nice, but I'm not surprised. You're the best thing that's ever happened to that boy."

"*We're* the best thing—the two of us. I'm glad our baby will have a big brother." She rubbed the small mound of her stomach. Suddenly, she remembered how anxious she'd been all day and jumped to her feet. "Well, don't keep me in suspense. What did Uncle Teedie say?"

Tyler casually set his coffee down and looped an arm over the back of the chair. "He thinks you're going to set the world on fire with your exposé. He says you're becoming a regular muckraker. Of course you still have to convince Mr. Bok to run it."

Chloe shrieked with excitement and reached down to wrap her arms around his neck. "Thank you, thank you, thank you." She was trying so hard to be obedient and abide by whatever Tyler thought was best concerning the story. *I don't know what I'd have done if he said no. Thank you, Lord, for changing his mind.*

He pulled her onto his lap and splayed his hand across her belly. "There's one condition though, we're leaving for D.C. as soon as you submit your story. Until then, you don't leave the house without Andrew or myself, understand?"

Chloe rose off his lap and braced her hands on her hips. "But why am I the prisoner? You're the one who foiled Morello's operation, not me. My article is ready, I could submit it today, but there's no way I'm ready to move yet." She looked around the kitchen. "I haven't even started packing in here."

Tyler got up and laid his hands on her shoulders. "Why is it no matter what kind of news I bring you, you have some objection?"

Chloe stamped her foot in frustration. It was a childish move. "You have no idea what it took me to get all those boxes in the parlor packed." She waved her hand in the air. "It wasn't magic, you know. I've decided I hate moving. If we're going to Washington, we're staying and putting down roots there."

Tyler moved to the cupboard and started unloaded its contents on the table. "I tell you what, TR released me of my duties until the day before the inauguration so I'm all yours. I've already arranged for Molly to come back and help. I don't know why you dismissed her in the first place."

Chloe didn't know why, either. The woman was a huge help and easy to get along with. Not about to admit her mistake, she raised her chin. "You know what they say about too many cooks in the kitchen. Besides, I thought you liked my cooking."

Tyler snorted and shook his head. "Woman, I see right through you. You're not about to get me on that one. Why don't you do the cooking and let Molly do the packing? I'll be around to lift anything heavy and you can even enlist Henry's help."

It was Chloe's turn to snort. "Not likely. He's not happy about moving away from his new friends. I've tried packing his room, and he unpacks it."

"I'll talk to him man to man. Why don't you go rest? Tomorrow I'll take you down to the magazine office and we go from there."

Chloe was tired. The stress of writing her story, dealing with moving, and her continued bouts of coughing had drained her reserves of energy. "Supper's in the oven. If you'll see that the table is set, I think I will lie down for a quick nap. Andrew should be here around five and it looks like the Lansing boys will be joining us before the three musketeers head back to their house." She moved to the doorway. "Oh, and don't let them talk you into any of that pie, it's for dessert tonight."

Tyler decided to load the stuff he'd piled on the table. Not seeing any boxes or crates, he stepped out the back door and headed to the small shed where they'd stacked the crates they'd moved to New York with.

The busted latch hung down, splinters of wood from the frame littered the ground. He opened the door cautiously and peeked in. The shed was dark and empty. Tyler kneeled to study the doorframe. It had definitely been jimmied.

The box forgotten, he stood and moved back toward the house looking for anything out of the ordinary. In a few long strides, he stood below the kitchen window. The snow was trampled down. On the fresh surface off to one side, he found the perfect imprint of a man's boot. His blood ran cold.

FRAGILE REPRIEVE

CHAPTER 28

Tyler planned to let Chloe sleep as long as possible. He wanted to show Andrew his discovery without worrying her. He rang him up and asked him to come over right away. Now he paced the front hall, waiting for Andrew's arrival. When the big man's shadow filled the glass in the door, Tyler threw it open.

"I'm glad I caught you before you could ring the bell. Chloe's sleeping and I don't want to wake her."

Andrew stepped inside and started to take off his coat.

"Leave it on. I have something to show you out back." Tyler grabbed his own coat, and they moved through the house and out the kitchen door to the small backyard. "I found this a while ago." He indicated the footprint in the snow.

Andrew kneeled down and spread his large hand across the imprint. "It's a man's for sure. Must have been trying to get in through the window." He stood. His head level with the bottom of the windowsill. "Looks like someone tried to jimmy the latch. The paint's scraped away."

Tyler stretched to his tiptoes. He still couldn't see over the lip. "I can't see that high and I'm six foot. That means unless there's another Goliath walking around, our guy must have used something to climb on. He probably broke into the shed looking for a ladder."

Andrew headed to the side of the brownstone. "Since you're an end unit, we only have three sides to consider. Let's check it out."

They found nothing in the narrow walkway between the buildings. The front steps and sidewalk set close to a street lamp. Tyler studied the street in both directions. It was a quiet residential area, where neighbors looked out for each other. "I don't think anyone would be stupid enough to try and come through the front. You thinking what I'm thinking?"

"Yeah, Morello's sniffing around. He must have figured out where you live. The street talk is the man is big on revenge."

Tyler climbed the steps. "Let's go inside and get out of this cold." They were hanging their coats up when Hank and his friends came charging down the stairs. "Sh, Miss Chloe's sleeping." He admonished the trio.

All three clamored to a stop. Hank frowned and muttered, "Sorry."

The other two boys stood on the bottom step, their mouths hanging open. "Wow, you weren't joshin', he is a giant." Jimmy said and took a big swallow.

Noah stepped up to Andrew and stuck his thumbs under his suspends. "You must eat a lot. In fact, I bet you could eat a whole cow all by yourself."

Andrew tipped his head back and roared with laughter. Remembering what Tyler had just said, he clamped his lips together and got down on one knee to be closer to eye level with the ten-year-old. "Tried that once. Made myself sick. Now pie is a whole other story. I can down me two or three of those pretty easy."

Hank shouldered his young friend out of the way. "Well, ma only made the one, so you have to share with the rest of us."

Andrew busted out laughing again. Tyler joined in until a sobering thought crossed his mind. "Hank, did you boys happen to see any strangers hanging around the neighborhood in the last day or so?"

The three boys looked at each other and shrugged. Hank shook his head. "Nah, I don't think so."

Jimmy nudged him. "What about that guy we saw in the alley yesterday? He wasn't from around here."

Tyler stiffened. The boy might unknowingly hold vital information. He sat down on the third step and settled his long bent legs on the floor, then pulled Jimmy up between them. "Son, can you remember what the man looked like? What he was wearing or carrying?"

Jimmy gave Hank a concerned look. Hank patted his friend's arm. "It's all right. My pa's a detective like Sherlock Holmes." He turned to Tyler. "You lookin' for clues to somethun?"

Tyler noticed Hank referred to him as pa. *Chloe's right, it feels good.* There was no time to think about that. Right now, it was crucial he learned everything he could about the stranger. "Jimmy, think back. What color was the man's hair? Did he have a mustache or a beard?"

"He had a hat on so I couldn't see his hair. His mustache was black or dark brown, so were his eyes. They were mean looking."

Tyler looked from Jimmy to Andrew. The idea that the kids were close enough to see the man's eyes made him cringe.

"Was he dressed like a workman or a businessman?" Andrew asked.

Hank fingered his own shirt. "He weren't no businessman, that's for sure. Had on regular clothes, not ragged, like he was poor. He was wearin' a coat like those men down on the docks wear. Had one arm tucked inside his coat like he was holdin' somethun he didn't want us to see."

❧

"Who?"

Everyone turned toward Chloe at the top of the stairs. Tyler let go of Jimmy and climbed to his feet. "I didn't hear you. Did you sleep well?"

Chloe ignored the question. "Who were you all talking about?" She saw the guarded look Tyler and Andrew exchanged. Something was going on and they were afraid to tell her. She planted a smile on her face. "Henry, you boys run up and put your game away. Pick up all your soldiers too, and then get washed up for dinner."

The three scurried past her. As soon as they were out of earshot, she repeated her question. "Which one of you is going to tell me who you were talking about?"

Andrew heaved up to his feet. "You might as well tell her, she isn't going to leave it alone until you do."

Tyler scowled at him, then looked at Chloe as she came the rest of the way down the stairs. "The boys saw a man in the alley and we found evidence that someone was trying to break in."

Chloe's pulse quickened. She put a hand to her throat and grabbed hold of the railing with the other. "You think it was Morello?"

Tyler reached out and helped her down the last two steps. "No. He'd never do his own dirty work. Especially if he thought he'd get caught."

"My guess it was one of his hired thugs." Andrew offered. "Probably sent him down here to snoop around, and the man decided to take a closer look."

Chloe rubbed her wrists, remembering the ropes that bound them, then put her hand on Tyler's chest above his heart. Even through his shirt, she could feel the raised scar from his bullet wound and the surgery that saved his life. Fear quivered in her belly. *Please Lord, no more.*

CHAPTER 29

Chloe reached over. Tyler's side of the bed was cold and empty. She struggled up on her elbows. "Tyler?" There was no answer. She flung off the blankets, scooted over the side, and grabbed up her robe. Sliding her feet into her slippers, she padded to the closed door and listened at the panel. The silence seemed ominous and brooding, like a storm about the break.

With a slow twist of the glass knob, she pulled it open enough to peek out. The hallway was dark and quiet. She stepped across to Hank's room and eased his door open. Moonlight filtered through the curtains and fell over the sleeping form of the boy. Chloe's heart swelled. She already loved him more than she thought possible. "Lord, protect my son."

Henry sighed in his sleep and rolled over. A book slid to the floor and closed. She tiptoed in and picked up the well-worn publication. Held up to the light of the moon, Chloe could make out the words 'The Memoirs of Sherlock Holmes'. She ran her hand over the gold lettering. It was one of her father's favorite books. When Henry found it in a box and asked to keep it, she didn't have the heart to refuse him. Holding the volume to her chest, she smiled down at the boy, knowing how much her father would have loved his new grandson. *I wish you were still here.*

A far away thud directed her attention to the hall. She sat the book down and raced out of the room. From the top of the stairs, she saw a light dance across the hallway floor. It was coming from the dining room. Voices floated up to her. "Tyler," she whispered, and waited. There was no answer.

Careful to plant her feet along the edge of each step closest to the wall, she crept down the staircase. The voices shifted and melted away with the light. *They're in the kitchen.* As she was about to round the corner into the dining room, something moved in her peripheral vision. Turning, she pressed her back against the wall and brought a hand up to cover her mouth as a cough began to build.

A shape silhouetted by the streetlamp darkened the frosted glass on the upper half of the front door, just feet away. She froze, stifling the urge to cough. Her eyes watched the brass knob slowly turn one way and then the other. *Dear God, what do I do?* Her eyes searched the dark hallway for a weapon and landed on the umbrella stand.

Taking a deep breath, she moved silently to the other side of the hall and pulled Tyler's cane from the stand. Brandishing the silver-knobbed handle, she eased back toward the relative safety of the parlor.

The door handle rattled as if in frustration. The shadowy figure moved and filled the sidelight. Chloe gasped as the blurry shape of a face pressed against the frosted glass. A large hand covered her mouth. Another wrapped around her waist and pulled her backwards into the parlor. *God, help me!* She swung the cane with both hands and connected with the side of her assailant's head.

"Ouch, Chloe, stopped it, it's me!" Tyler hissed in her ear. He dropped his hand from her mouth.

She swung around and fell against his chest. "There's someone trying to get in the front door."

Andrew stepped past them. They heard him throw the door open and rush down the steps.

Tyler held her out at arm's length. "Are you okay? What were you doing downstairs wielding my cane like some kind of ancient warrior?"

Now that the threat was over, Chloe started trembling uncontrollably. "I woke up and couldn't find you then I heard a noise downstairs so I came down to investigate."

"The noise was your cat. Magic knocked over a box in the kitchen. Andy and I agreed to take turns standing guard. It was his turn first, but I couldn't sleep."

Andrew lumbered into the room, shivering and shaking off snow. "Whoever it was, most have gotten spooked. All I found were footprints in the fresh snow and this." He held up a tin of kerosene.

"That settles it. Pack a bag. I'm moving you and Henry into a hotel. We'll hire someone to pack everything else up."

Chloe started to interrupt. "But…"

He held up a finger. "I know what you're going to say, so just let me finish. You and I will be waiting to see Mr. Bok at the Journal when it opens. Once that's taken care of I'll bring you back here, and we'll oversee the packing together." He turned to his friend. "Andrew, would you take charge of Hank in the morning? I'll write down the Lansing's address. I'd prefer he not be underfoot tomorrow, but I want to know he's safe."

"Sure thing. I'll take him to the Natural History Museum. That should take up most of the day. If not, we'll wing it from there."

Things were moving so fast Chloe's head was spinning. Tyler and Andrew both looked at her as if expecting an argument. Maybe it was being pregnant or just the emotional rollercoaster of the past few months. Whatever it was, Chloe was drained. Her hands came up in surrender. "As long as the Journal gets my story and all my men are safe, I'm fine with getting out of here as soon as possible."

❧

Tyler was prepared for her chin to come up and her willfulness to surface. The fact that she conceded so easily showed just how scared she really was. He pulled her into his arms and held her close. "I'm not going to let anything happen to you, Hank, or the baby." He whispered into her hair as his chin rested on top of her head. "Let's get that bag packed."

A look passed between him and Andrew. The man nodded once and headed to the kitchen. Tyler trusted him to deal with securing the house and guarding them until they could leave.

It was almost midnight, not too late to call TR, who was probably devouring another book. The man was insatiable when it came to reading and could go through two or three books a day. Tyler used the phone in the upstairs hallway while Chloe gathered a few belongings for them.

An irritated voice answered. "This better be important, I was at a bully good part."

Tyler kept his voice low. "TR, its Tyler. Someone tried to get in the house tonight. He got scared off. I'm moving Chloe and Hank to the Iroquois down on West Forty-fourth. It's new and should have good security. Could you send a coach over? I don't want to chance it trying to hail a hack at this hour."

Roosevelt huffed his disapproval of the whole matter. "By George, these hooligans are making me angry. I wish I had more time here to settle this. Hopefully, Ben Odell will get the job done. Meanwhile, I call up Devery and let him know what's going on. I'll have my personal coach at your door in half an hour."

"Thank you, sir."

"And son, I'll be praying for the safety of your family."

Tyler rang off, feeling better and more in control.

CHAPTER 30

The day broke in a bluster of March winds rattling the panes in the window Tyler stood before. Below him on Pennsylvania Avenue, the crowds were gathering in anticipation. McKinley's swearing in and inaugural address would take place on the steps of the US Capital, but first there would be a parade down Pennsylvania passed the Willard Hotel. He'd gotten rooms on the third floor so Chloe and Hank could watch the festivities in comfort.

Chloe came up and wove her arm through his. "Did you ever in your wildest dreams, imagine you'd be standing next to the vice president when he is sworn into office?"

"Never. My folks would be very proud of their only son."

"Well, I'm pretty proud of my only husband. When do we leave for the Senate Building?"

Tyler pulled out his father's pocket watch. "Actually, we should be going soon. Is Hank ready?"

"He's been ready for an hour. I've never seen a kid more excited to dress up and set in a stuffy room with a bunch of stogy old politicians."

He turned around and gathered Chloe in his arms. "Maybe our son is destined to be a force on Capitol Hill someday."

"Maybe he'll make me the mother of the president." She grinned up at him, her single dimple indenting her smooth cheek. He leaned down and kissed the hollow and then her lips. "Mm, did I ever tell you what a good kisser you are, Mr. Reynolds?"

He put on his most skeptical look. "Are you speaking from your vast experience or just taking a wild guess?"

Chloe giggled. "Kiss me again and I'll tell you the truth."

He bent and lifted her into his arms. The scent of lavender and soap filled his nostrils. His lips sought and found hers.

"Ah, gee whiz, do you guys have to be doing that all the time? I'm an impressionable kid, you know."

Tyler tipped his forehead to hers. "We've been caught—again."

"I guess you had better put me down."

Tyler lowered her to the floor and turned to the boy standing in the doorway. "Polite young men knock before entering a room."

Hank blushed and lowered his head. "I forgot. Sorry." He pulled on the stiff collar of his new suit. "Can we leave yet? I don't know how much longer I can stand this stinkin' collar."

Chloe hid a chuckle behind her hand and whispered. "So much for our future politician."

The night's festivities were in full swing. Chloe sat with Edith Roosevelt and her stepdaughter Alice and watched the couples waltz by. "I so glad I have the excuse of pregnancy so I can set a few of these out. My feet are sore from being stepped on."

"I'd much rather not be here at all," seventeen-year-old Alice declared. "I prefer Manhattan. It's much more gay and lively."

Chloe glanced over in time to see Edith give the girl a scathing look. A general animosity between the two filled the air with tension.

Mrs. Roosevelt harrumphed her disdain. "A young lady in your position is expected to conduct herself in a certain fashion. You would do good to follow Chloe's example."

Trying to diffuse the situation, Chloe smiled at the teenager. "I'm not much for big society parties either, but I support my husband and look up to your father, so I do my best to make them proud."

A sad look frittered across Alice's face and was quickly replaced by one of indifference. "My father doesn't care a twit for me so it makes no never mind. Now if I had a husband as handsome as yours, I'd bend over backwards to make him happy."

Alice looked past Chloe's shoulder. "Speaking of the devil." She pasted on a charming smile. "So you came back to rescue your beautiful wife. I wish someone would rescue me."

Chloe looked up at the touch of Tyler's hand on her bare shoulder. He still had the ability to send electric shocks through her system.

Tyler ignored Alice's pouty face and gave a slight bow to the two women. "Excuse me, ladies, I came to steal my wife away for one last dance before we call it an evening."

Chloe stood. "It's been a wonderful day and so good to see you again Alice. Mrs. Roosevelt, I've already expressed my congratulations to Uncle Teedie, but I hope you know I include you in them. I think you'll be a great addition to the White House."

Mrs. Roosevelt fanned herself and smiled pleasantly. "My dear, as always, it's been a pleasure. Now that we'll both be living in DC, we'll have to be sure and spend some time together."

Alice gave an elaborate yawn. "I'm suddenly very tire." She looked up at Tyler and gave him a coquettish smile. "Do you suppose you and Chloe could allow me to catch a ride with you when you're ready to go? Father will be here forever and I don't think I can stand dancing with another half-dead old codger."

Tyler smiled, totally unaware of the tense undercurrents at the table. "Of course. Having a lovely lady on each arm will make me the envy of every man in the place. We'll stop back by for you after this dance."

"You probably shouldn't have done that." Chloe warned, as he guided her to the dance floor.

"Done what? I was a perfect gentleman." He swung her around into position for the next waltz.

"Couldn't you feel the tension between those two? Alice is jealous of her stepmother and craves her father's attention. And, although I think Edith cares for her, she doesn't know how to handle such a spirited, head-strong young girl. You may have just picked the wrong side."

Tyler looked completely lost. "I didn't know I was picking a side. I thought I was doing the gentlemanly thing by escorting the girl home."

A couple of lavish twirls brought Chloe back into his arms again. "Maybe you're right. Hopefully, that's how Edith sees it too."

The dance over, Tyler and Chloe found Alice waiting for them near the coat-check room. Enveloped in a gorgeous blonde ankle-length fur, the teen gave them a mischievous smile. "I thought I'd save you the trouble of pulling me out of the clutches of my step-mother and meet you here. I've already sent the woman looking for you coats."

"Thank you for being so thoughtful. I really am ready to get off my feet."

Alice snorted a laugh. "Being thoughtful has nothing to do with it. I wanted to duck out, and you provided me with an acceptable escort."

Chloe was glad the ride back to the Willard Hotel was quiet and uneventful. She could barely keep her eyes open. It had been a busy week of house hunting, organizing painters and movers, and getting ready for the inauguration. The private brougham pulled up in front of the hotel entrance and a liveried doorman extended the steps and opened the door. Alice made no move to exit, even though she was closest to the door.

"You can go first, dear." Chloe said.

Alice snuggled deeper into her fur. "Oh, I'm fine. I'm not getting out here."

"Oh, I didn't realize you weren't staying here with the rest of your father's party." Chloe wasn't sure how to handle the situation. She wasn't the girl's mother or guardian and she didn't imagine Alice would listen to her, anyway. "Perhaps you'd like to come up to our suite for a cup of coffee. We could even order some dessert."

Tyler took the matter into his own hands. "Alice, it's too late for a beautiful, young girl like yourself to be out alone. You left with us. That makes Chloe and I responsible for your safety, and I don't relish losing my job because I didn't watch out for you. I'd appreciate it if you'd come in with us."

The girl gave him a sidelong look. A coquettish smile played across her face. "I wouldn't want to cause you any trouble, Tyler, darling." She faked a yawn. "It is rather late and I have an early engagement with a couple of friends to go boating tomorrow." She extended a hand. "Could you be a dear and help me down?"

Tyler shifted forward and handed her off to the waiting doorman, then turned to Chloe. "That was rather awkward."

Chloe smiled and squeezed his arm. "You handled her beautifully. Of course, it helps that she thinks you're handsome."

Tyler twitched an eyebrow up and down and pretended to twirl his mustache. "You play your cards right and I'll show you how beautifully I can handle you."

CHAPTER 31

Washington DC proved to be more than Tyler bargained for, and yet he was restless. The political byplay of constant hobnobbing, bootlicking, and backslapping made him cringe. TR felt much the same way. His duties as vice president amounted to busy work—something he was not good at.

Roosevelt stood at the window with his back to the room. "What's on the agenda for today?"

Tyler scanned the appointment book in his lap, even though he already knew what was written there. "You have a luncheon at eleven with representatives of The Women's Christian Temperance Union. It seems the WCTU is petitioning to prohibit golf on Sundays and they're looking for your support."

"Balderdash! I couldn't care less if rich men play golf on Sundays. Next they'll want to close down boxing, shooting, and every other sport that gets my blood moving. Can you get me out of it?"

"No, you're already committed. Besides, these ladies are becoming a force to be reckoned with not just here in the US but worldwide. It would behoove you to have them on your side.

"After the luncheon, you're meeting with a contingent of librarians who want to honor you as America's most voracious reader." Tyler's exasperated sigh must have been louder than he realized.

TR turned and stomped around the desk. "I agree. What a bloody waste of time. I'm beginning to think I should have never let Henry Lodge talk me into going to the Republican convention. If I'd followed my instincts I'd still be Governor of New York and actually accomplishing something." TR picked up a framed photograph of his Colorado mountain lion hunt. "I would a great deal rather be anything than vice president but it is what it is."

Tyler didn't express his thoughts, although he agreed with the man. *I feel like a glorified secretary. Something needs to change.*

❦

Chloe roamed from room to room in their new Georgetown townhouse. It was a nice enough place with four narrow stories in a row of similar federal-style homes. They were only leasing, which was good since she didn't like Washington in the least. *This will never be home.*

Her pregnancy was progressing well—at least she thought so. Her new doctor, Samuel Brewster, didn't like the cough she'd developed or the fact that she'd only gained a mere five pounds. She didn't tell him how fatigued she got doing everyday chores or how she got short of breath on her daily trips up and down the flights of stairs of their new home.

It was early April. The snow had given way to green buds and crocus. Chloe donned a light shawl and ventured out to take a stroll. She hoped to intercept Henry on his way home from school and enlist him to go to the local market with her to pick up baking supplies.

She had gone three blocks when a bout of coughing seized her. Doubled over, she braced herself against the wrought iron banister of a stately Georgian-style house.

A young maid opened the front door and hurried down the steps. "Madam, are you okay?"

Chloe managed to squelch the need to cough. "Could I have a drink of water, please?"

The girl hurried back inside and returned with a half-filled glass. Chloe was taking her last swallow when Henry came running up.

He dropped down beside her and took her hand. "What's the matter? Are you sick? Is it the baby?"

Chloe handed the glass back to the maid. "Thank you." She looked from the girl to Henry. "I'm okay now. It was just a little coughing spell." She climbed to her feet, not letting go of the railing until she was sure of her balance. Lethargy like she'd never felt before overcame her. Suddenly she wanted nothing more than to climb into her bed and sleep. "I was going to have you help me carry some groceries home from the market, but I think maybe we'd better not today." She wrapped an arm around Henry's shoulders and smiled to distract him. "How was school?"

He shrugged. "It was okay, I guess. Old man Bender sent three kids to the principal's office." He mimicked the teacher. "I will *not* tolerate wisenheimers in my classroom."

"It's Mr. Bender and I hope you were not one of the culprits."

Henry ducked his head. "Nah, I actually kinda like history class. He tells us a lot of swell stuff. Did you know Mr. Roosevelt led a bunch of guys called the Rough Riders up some hill on an island called Cuba." Henry brought up an invisible rifle and started firing. "Poomb! Poomb!"

Chloe couldn't help but laugh at his enthusiasm. "I'll bet you didn't know my father provided the carbines and revolvers they used. I think papa would have liked to have gone with him had he been twenty years younger and didn't have a daughter to raise."

Henry's eyes rounded. "Wow! So is he like my grandpa or somethun?"

"Yes, I guess he would be." A thought struck her. "Henry, would you like Mr. Tyler and I to officially adopt you so you'd have our last name?"

"Really?" He puffed out his chest and put his thumbs under his suspenders. "I'd be Henry Alonzo Reynolds." He grinned up at her. "I like it. It sounds important."

"Well then, tonight we'll talk to Mr. Tyler and tomorrow he can get the ball rolling."

Chloe watched from where she sat next to an open window while Henry waited on the front stoop. "There he is!" the boy shouted and jumped up to get the door of the open-topped carriage. "Miss Chloe says I can be your for real son. Henry Reynolds, how do you like that?"

Tyler stepped down out of the carriage. He smiled up at Chloe in the window and plopped his derby on Hank's head. "Well, that sounds like just the ticket to me. The new baby is going to need an official big brother. When did you come up with this idea?"

"Today. We were walking home after Miss Chloe got over her coughing spell and she was telling me about her pa being kinda like my grandpa."

Tyler stiffened and looked back up at the window. Chloe was gone. He stopped the boy on the sidewalk. "Miss Chloe had a coughing spell? Where were you two?"

Hank took the hat off and twirled it on his hand like he'd seen Tyler do. "She came to meet me from school so I could carry groceries. 'cept we didn't go to the market 'cause she had a coughin' fit. I think that means we're not having dessert. She didn't bake nothing."

A feeling of dread crept over Tyler. He'd woke up several times during the night lately to find her in the bathroom coughing. She'd said it was just a spring cold. Now he wasn't so sure. "Let go see if she needs any help, okay?"

They found her in the kitchen stirring a pot of stew. "There you are. Just in time. I think we'll eat in here tonight." She smiled at Tyler like nothing was wrong. "So Henry shared our idea with you. What do you think?"

Tyler grabbed the stack of bowls off the table and carried them to the stove. He kissed her forehead. *It feels warm.* "Let me do this. You go set down." He put the bowls down and took the ladle from her.

She acted as if nothing was the matter and, except for being a bit pale, she seemed fine. Tyler wasn't satisfied. Before the night was over, he would find out what was going on.

CHAPTER 32

"It's just a cold." Chloe stated nonchalantly, as if it didn't worry 'her as well. "Besides, I saw my new doctor two weeks ago. I'm pregnant, not dying, for goodness sakes. I don't need to run to him every month." She continued smoothing lotion onto her arms. "So how hard will it be to officially adopt Henry?"

"You're changing the subject. You're going back to see Dr. Brewster and I'm going with you this time." Tyler came up behind her and wrapped his arms around her expanding waist. Head bent, he nuzzled her ear and neck. His breath tickled. Chloe pulled her shoulder up against the sensation.

She looked at him in the mirror. "If I promise to see the doctor tomorrow, will you check into the necessary paperwork we'll need to file for adoption?"

He rested his chin on her shoulder and looked back at her reflection. "Nope, I'm going with you. I can get the ball rolling on the adoption after I drop you back here. That way I'll know you're not hiding anything from me." His eyes took on a troubled look. "I'm not letting anything happen to you or our baby, and if I don't know what's going on, I can't do anything about it."

Chloe leaned back and kissed the underside of his chin, his dark stubble brushing her lips. "I love you, Tyler

Reynolds, but you aren't responsible for saving the world. That's God's job."

❦

The morning dawned with the sweet smell of spring. As soon as Henry headed off the school, Tyler hailed a cab and the two headed to Doctor Brewster's office off Dupont Circle. They had to wait while he finished with his first patient before he was able to see them.

"What seems to be the problem?" He asked over the top of her file.

Before Chloe could reply, Tyler spoke up. "She's having heavy bouts of coughing, weakness, fatigue, fever, and I don't think she's eating enough."

"I'm probably just overdoing. I keep telling him this is typical during pregnancy, but he won't listen."

Samuel Brewster frowned. He pushed the spectacles up his nose and tapped a pen against the folder in his hand. "Hmm, more coughing and have you had any shortness of breath and dizziness?"

Chloe didn't want to admit it in front of Tyler, but she couldn't lie. "Some. I figured it's just the baby pressing up against my lungs."

"Let's get a sputum sample and I want to listen to your lungs. Mr. Reynolds, please send in my nurse when you go out."

Tyler leaned against the wall and crossed his arms. "I'm not going anywhere."

Dr. Brewster pursed his lips and shrugged. "Suit yourself."

The exam over, Tyler and Chloe waited in the doctor's office for his return. Anxious and nervous at what the man might say, Chloe chewed her bottom lip and bowed her head to say a quiet prayer.

Tyler's voice cut into her desperate thoughts. "Lord, we don't yet know what the problem is, but you do."

Chloe stole a look at her husband. His head was bent. His eyes squeezed tight. She closed her own and let him pray.

"Whatever is wrong, you can fix it, and that's what I'm asking for. I've never asked for much, but this is important so please see your way clear to keep my wife and baby healthy."

Before he could go on, the door opened, and Dr. Brewster stepped in. Chloe gripped Tyler's hand. She couldn't seem to swallow as she searched the physician's face. He didn't hide his emotions well. His lips formed a grim line. His eyes looked troubled.

One elbow braced on the desk, Tyler asked around the fist he had pressed against his mouth. "Well, what's your prognosis?"

This is it. Please, God, let my baby be okay. Chloe's fingernails bit into Tyler's skin. She wrapped her other hand around their joined hands to keep it from shaking.

The man expelled a nose full of air. Taking his glasses off, he rubbed the indents at the bridge, then slid them back into place. "First of all, let me stress that science is not perfect and I will need to do additional tests. The fact that you are pregnant means I will not take any x-rays, which is the definitive test for diagnosing a variety of conditions."

He laced his fingers together and looked at Chloe. "There's no easy way to say this, so I'm going to give it to you straight. I believe you have early onset tuberculosis. What form it has taken is the question. My prognosis would be tuberculous adrenalitis and or extrapulmonary tuberculosis."

Chloe couldn't form words to ask questions. Her mind couldn't seem to wrap itself around what the doctor was saying. The only thought she had was of the baby. One hand captured in Tyler's, she draped the other across her stomach. *My baby! Oh, God, my baby!*

❧

Tyler found his voice. It came out in a raspy whisper. "Could you please say that again in layman's terms? What is happening to my wife and child?"

Dr. Brewster focused on Tyler. "Have you ever heard of consumption?"

"Yes, of course. It's a poor man's disease. Is that what this is?"

"In the broad sense, yes. The medical community still does not understand all the various types of tuberculosis, but strides are being taken in combating it."

Tyler wanted to ask the right questions, but wasn't sure what they were. "So it is treatable. My wife will be okay?"

Dr. Brewster licked his lips. "I need to conduct more tests before I can give you an opinion. I'm sorry. As you may already know, TB can be highly contagious. Just as a precaution, I want to move Chloe to the isolation ward at Columbia Hospital for Women. Once all the tests are in, we can set down and determine the best course of action."

He started to stand when Chloe lifted her head and whispered. "What about my baby?"

The desperate, terrified look on her face threatened to rip Tyler's heart right out of his chest. "Chloe, darling, our baby will be fine." He didn't know if that was true or not, but he had to offer her something—some shred of comfort.

Chloe abruptly pulled her hand out of his and stood to slam her palms down on the desktop. "I don't want platitudes. I want to know if my child is going to be okay."

Tyler got to his feet and reached out to her. Without looking at him, she put a hand out to stop him. "No, Tyler. I need an answer. Dr. Brewster, will I deliver a healthy baby?"

"Mrs. Reynolds, tuberculosis is bacterial in nature. With proper treatment, close monitoring, a healthy regimen of diet and exercise, I believe your baby has a good chance of being born healthy. Had you waited until after delivery to see me about your symptoms, my prognosis would be entirely different."

Chloe visibly wilted. Tyler caught her to him. "Doctor, could you give us a minute, please?"

"Certainly, I need to make arrangements for your admittance, anyway. Take as long as you need." He quietly closed the door behind him as he left the room.

Tyler sat back down and pulled Chloe into his lap. "Here, darling." He gave her his handkerchief. "We need to think positive. We've been through a lot of tough times, we'll weather this one as well. Besides, we have God on our side."

She lifted her head and looked up at him with eyes swimming in tears. "Do you really think so? If it were you, I'd know you would pull through okay. You're so much stronger than me. And it's not really about me. It's about our baby. Oh, Tyler, she just has to be okay."

Looking for something to brighten the moment, he grabbed on to her last words. "She, huh? You think it's going to be a girl?"

Chloe gave him a trembling smile. "Somehow, I've felt it since she first started kicking."

Tyler pulled her head to his chest and smoothed her hair. "I've always wanted a daughter."

CHAPTER 33

Dr. Brewster came into Chloe's hospital room. His expression hadn't changed much in the five days she'd been in the hospital. "Mrs. Reynolds, will your husband be coming soon?"

"He'll be here later this morning. Do you finally have news for us?"

He stood beside her bed, clipboard in hand. "Well, yes, but I'd like to speak with your husband as well."

Chloe's temper rose a notch. "Dr. Brewster, I'm a full grown woman. Just because I'm married doesn't make me any less capable of understanding and making decisions concerning my own body."

The color leached from the man's face, then returned to bloom a rosy hue. "I'm so sorry, Mrs. Reynolds, I didn't intend to imply your intelligence was in any way inferior to your husband's. I just thought it would be easier to share my findings with both of you together as I have a busy day ahead and may not be available later."

It was Chloe's turn to blush. "I'm sorry I jumped to conclusions. It's just that I've been cooped up here imagining all kinds of terrible things."

Samuel Brewster smiled and patted Chloe's hand. "Quite all right. I can understand how you must be feeling. I would like to wait for your husband, but I will tell you this. It isn't as dire as I first thought." He gave her a wink and turned to the door. "Why don't I have a nurse ring Mr. Reynolds up and see if he can come early so we can all discuss this and come up with a plan?"

"Thank you, Doctor. That would be wonderful." Chloe lay back against the pillow and closed her eyes. "It's not so bad. My baby and I are going to be okay. Thank you, Jesus!"

Chloe waited for over an hour. Antsy and nervous, she got out of bed and was pacing the small room when Tyler rushed in, looking disheveled and anxious.

"Whoa, slow down, Cowboy. You look like you ran all the way here."

"I did." He gasped. "I was at the courthouse. There must be a major trial going on, I couldn't get a hack to even look in my direction so I hoofed it. What's going on? Are you okay? The nurse said the doctor needed to see me right away."

Chloe poured him a glass of water. "Here. It's a clean glass. I haven't used it." She worked her bottom up onto the side of the bed, her feet dangling. "I'm fine, just bored out of my mind. Doctor Brewster has the results of my tests and wants to discuss them with both of us. Do the nurses know you're here?"

Tyler harrumphed. "I raced past their station like a madman. I don't know how they could have missed me." He settled beside her and placed his hand on her belly. "How's Emily doing today?"

"Emily?"

Tyler shrugged. "Well, I figured if you're so sure it's a girl, she should have a name and I thought you'd want to name her after your mother."

Chloe reached up and pulled his face down to plant a loud kiss on his lips. "You are the most wonderful man." A sudden idea came to her. "Let's name her Emily Rose Reynolds so she has both our mother's names."

Tyler smoothed a stray strand of hair from Chloe's face. "That sounds perfect."

Dr. Brewster cleared his throat at the door. "I hope I'm not interrupting anything." He came forward and shook Tyler's hand. "Mr. Reynolds, I glad you could come so quickly. I know your wife is anxious to learn my findings." He pulled up a chair opposite them and tapped the file in his hands. "I have good news and bad news.

"The results show that you indeed have active tuberculosis, but it's of the Pleurisy strain meaning it can be curable over time with the right treatment. Thank goodness, we caught it in its early stages so it will be easier to combat. The bad news is you also may have adrenal insufficiency, likely Addison's disease."

"Likely? So you don't know for sure?" Tyler asked.

"Well, your wife is presenting with all the classic symptoms; fatigue, muscle weakness, and low blood pressure causing dizziness. Since these are many of the same symptoms of pregnancy, they often go unnoticed. It was the unusual darkening of her skin that first alerted me to the possibility of Addison's.

Tyler's arm tightened around Chloe's shoulder. "And it's treatable, correct?"

"Don't get me wrong, Mr. Reynolds, this has the potential to be very serious and you will have to make some huge adjustments, one of which will mean a move to a sanatorium for you, Mrs. Reynolds."

"But we just moved to DC and besides expecting a baby, we're adopting a boy." She looked up at Tyler for support. "We can do this, can't we?"

Tyler smiled down at her. "Of course, we'll find you the best sanatorium in the capitol."

Dr. Brewster interrupted. "I'm afraid that's impossible. The closest Tubercular sanatorium is in upstate New York and although it's a good place, I don't personally recommend it. Mrs. Reynolds, if you want to get your health back as quickly as possible, I would advise you to consider a drier climate where the air is clean. My choice would be The Glockner Sanatorium in Colorado Springs, Colorado. The Sisters of Charity have become world renown for their care and treatment of Tubercular patients."

"Colorado Springs! I have family there." She turned to Tyler. The first ray of hope after a dismal week brought a smile to her face. "Oh, Tyler, I—we could see Auntie Clare and Abel again." Emotion choked her. She hadn't realized how much she missed and needed their support. It would mean another move, across the country this time.

Tyler kissed her forehead and turned to the doctor. "Can you make the arrangements? We can be there within the week."

Visibly relieved, the doctor nodded his head. "I was hoping you'd agreed. I truly believe this is the best course of action, and to have a support system already in place will help greatly. I'll arrange for your discharge.

"Mrs. Reynolds, you are contagious, so please stay out of the public as much as possible. It's thought that this disease is transferred through the air and by others using the same utensils, so you need to separate yourself as much as possible and wear a scarf or mask at all times. I'll contact Glockner and see if we can get you a room. I'll have my office call you with the specifics." He shook both their hands. "Now if you'll excuse me, I have a baby about ready to make an appearance."

As soon as the doctor left the room, Chloe fell into Tyler's arms. "I was so scared, imagining all kind of terrible things. I think everything will be okay, don't you?"

Tyler was still scared—terrified, in fact. He could not lose her or his daughter and would do everything in his power to ensure that. "I'm sure you're right." He smiled at her. "Now, I hate to leave you, but it looks like I have a lot to do."

Chloe gasped and stilled. "Your job! What about your job?"

Tyler hugged her close. "Don't you worry. Remember the doctor's orders—no stress. I'll take care of everything. I'll stop on my way out and talk to the nurses to see exacting when they'll have your discharge papers ready. You try to get some rest. I'll be back later to take you home."

He moved to kiss her. She ducked her head so that his lips landed on her forehead. He realized in that second they wouldn't be able to share that particular kind of intimate connection again. Choked up with raw emotion, he whispered, "I love you."

Once he left the hospital, he immediately headed back to the capital building and found TR in his office reading. In a burst of pent up worry, Tyler relayed all that was turning their lives upside down. Raking his hands through his hair, he stopped his pacing in front of the fireplace. "I don't know what I'm supposed to do."

Roosevelt finished off the cup of coffee before him and twirled the china saucer. "You take your wife and moved to Colorado, that's what you do. There's nothing to hold you here. In fact, I wish I was going with you. If I can't make anything happen soon, I'll probably go back to Sagamore Hill and spend time with Edie and the children."

"I hate to leave you when your vice presidency is just getting started."

TR snorted his disgust. "Hogwash. We both know this office is a showcase to do nothing that matters. There's no sense in both of us losing our minds in boredom." He got up and came around the desk. With a firm hand on Tyler's back, Roosevelt ushered him to the door. "You go to Colorado. That doctor is right. Good clean air, a dry climate, exercise, and a healthy diet is just the ticket to get Chloe back on her feet. It worked for me when I was a scrawny kid with asthma and look at me now. Colorado's one of my favorite places in this whole, blasted country so you can expect to see me on your doorstep at some point. Now get out of here and go take care of that beautiful wife of yours."

CHAPTER 34

Tyler secured a private sleeper for the three of them. Chloe seldom left it, even having her meals there. Hank had his face pressed against the glass for most of the trip. "I think I see a buffalo!"

Tyler leaned over and scanned the prairie that filled their view for miles. "That, my friend, is an antelope. A buffalo is several hundred pounds heavier and dark-colored. I doubt you'll be seeing any roaming free. They've been hunted almost to extinction." The train rounded a slow curve, bringing the Rocky Mountains into view.

"Would you look at that! They're so big! Like giant, jagged teeth rising up out of the ground. And people actually go across them?"

Tyler laughed at the boy's excitement and awe. He pointed to the south. "You see that really tall one there, that's Pikes Peak. We'll be living in the shadow of it in Colorado Springs."

"Wow! Can we climb to the top? I'll bet we can see clear back to New York from there."

Tyler looked over at Chloe's sleeping form. "Sh. Remember, she needs to rest."

"Sorry," Hank whispered. He sat back in his seat and grew pensive. "She's gonna be alright, isn't she? I already lost one ma and pa. I ain't—haven't got no hankerin' to lose another."

Tyler perched on the edge of the lower berth where Chloe rested. "I'm sorry we couldn't get the adoption taken care of before we left. Once we get settled, I'll make sure it happens, okay?"

Hank moved back to the window. "Sure." He was quiet for a moment, then turned to Tyler. "Would it be okay if I called you and Miss Chloe ma and pa now instead of waitin'? I figure everything's gonna be new for all of us so that way no one will know you're not my real parents."

Tyler's throat constricted. He managed to swallow the lump that quickly formed and replied. "Sounds like a perfect plan, buddy."

❧❧

Chloe blinked the tears away and lay still, facing the compartment wall. She had awakened to hear Tyler and Hank talking about the adoption. She knew the boy had lost his parents several years earlier, but other than to say they got sick and died, Henry never shared much about them. She closed her eyes. *Lord, please do not let that boy get hurt again.*

When she woke once more, they were pulling into Union Station in the heart of Denver. Tyler ushered them outside and hailed an opened top cab. "Brown Palace, please."

Chloe laid a hand on Tyler's up-stretched arm. "Are you sure we can afford to stay there? I mean, it's the fanciest place in town and you don't have a job anymore, remember."

"About that, I have an appointment with my old boss, James Archer."

The announcement caught her off guard. She remembered Mr. Archer from their conversation at the

Bassett Ranch when he questioned her about any relationships she had with members of the Wild Bunch. He was abrupt and cynical. She didn't like him much then and wasn't sure she wanted her husband to get tangled up with him again. "How did he know you were coming back to Colorado?"

"I called him." Tyler handed her up into the coach and climbed in beside her. Hank twisted around on the seat beside him to take in all the sights and sounds of Denver. He held up his hands in defense. "Look, I know what you're going to say. Working for Pinkerton's before wasn't a good idea. I was looking for a legal, justifiable way to get revenge against my parent's killers. They used me, but I used them too. I'm a different person now."

Chloe had to admit he had changed from the rough outlaw persona his undercover work required to the man she loved and admired. She also knew how close he came to losing himself to that life, and it scared her to think he would consider going back there. *I can't push him. He's doing this because of me. It has to be his decision.* She hoped she could find the right words.

"I have one thing for you to consider then I'll trust you to do what you think is right." She turned in the seat and looked up into his blue eyes. "First of all, you're a man that seeks justice and wants to right wrongs. I love that about you, but it has almost gotten you killed several times.

"I'm sure the Pinkerton Agency started out on high moral ground, but if Mr. Archer is an example of what principles they adhere to now, then I think you need to ask yourself an important question. Are you're willing to be associated with them and risk what we have now to be part of that again?"

Tyler twisted his mouth in thought, then gave her a reassuring smile. "How about I make you a promise? If at any point I think Archer isn't on the up and up or his tactics and motives are questionable, I'll step back and bow out." He brought her hand up to his lips. Turning it palm up, he kissed it. "You, Hank, and our baby are the most important things in the world to me. I don't intend to let anything get in the way of that."

As much as she didn't like it, Chloe would have to be happy with that. He had a two o'clock appointment, leaving them time to enjoy a delicious lunch together in the opulent dining room of Denver's most prestigious hotel. Henry could hardly keep his eyes in his head and his mouth only closed when he was stuffing it full of food.

"Slow down, mister, or you're going to make yourself sick." Chloe wagged a finger at him.

"I get hungry when I'm excited and this chicken-whatchamacallit is really good."

She laughed. "It's call Chicken Cordon bleu, which means blue ribbon chicken."

Henry talked around another bite. "It deserves a blue ribbon in my book."

Tyler and Chloe both laughed at his exuberance for the sophisticated dish. Tyler handed him a linen napkin. "A gentleman never talks with his mouth full, especially in a place like this. Here, wipe your face."

Henry took the fancy white cloth. "Thanks, pa."

Chloe's heart leaped. He said the words so easily and natural. She looked from Henry to Tyler. They had a special bond she wasn't a part of. It made her happy and sad at the same time. *I don't never want to see either one of them get hurt.*

❧❧

Tyler leaned forward in his chair. "Let me get this straight. You're offering me a position here in the Denver office with no undercover work involved?"

James Archer tipped back in his chair and rested his arms across his paunch. "Your call was unexpected, but it came at exactly the right time. I know how you feel about going back undercover, especially now that you're a married man. I also know what a first-rate agent you became for us. Pinkerton's recognizes and appreciates the excellent work you did in Philadelphia with those arson cases."

Tyler was speechless. "I have to admit, I'm a little shocked you'd even consider me. We both know what I did—going undercover as an outlaw and train robber—I did for all the wrong reasons." He rubbed his thigh. "If I hadn't been shot first, I would have killed at least a couple of men."

The director bent forward over his desk and picked up a paper from the stack in front of him. "The point is, that didn't happen. The scoundrels we caught that day were all wanted men. Except for Kid Curry, they're all serving time."

An instant dread spread through Tyler. The man he one time thought was responsible for his parent's murders was free? Harvey, 'Kid Curry' Logan didn't turn out to be their killer, but he was responsible for almost a dozen other deaths, a couple of them lawmen.

Tyler sat up straight. "What do you mean 'except for Curry'?"

Archer gave a disgusted sigh. "He escaped not long after we dragged him in. At the moment, his whereabouts is unknown. I imagine he's back riding with the Wild Bunch, although the word is Cassidy and Sundance have left the country, so maybe he's with some other gang."

Tyler didn't share what he knew about Butch and Sundance boarding a ship to South America, but the news about Logan rankled. In the months Tyler rode with the Wild Bunch, he'd come to despise Logan. The man was ruthless and as far as Tyler could tell, he didn't have a conscious either. It had taken everything in him not to pull his gun and free the world of the menace when he had the chance. Now the scum was free to wreak havoc on more innocent people.

Tension worked in his jaw. His fingers itched to hold the gun no longer strapped to his side. He was surprised at how intensely he felt. The law had always meant something special to him. That's why he became a lawyer in the first place. He had been happy with his career before his parent's murders, but his experience as a Pinkerton agent chasing and running with true outlaws changed all that. He had to admit even his time investigating the arson cases in Philadelphia or working for TR didn't offer the same kind of excitement and challenge.

Tyler looked back at his former boss. "Do you want me to go after him?"

Archer waved a hand. "No. No. We have other men on the Curry case. Listen Reynolds, I know you're aware the men responsible for killing your folks were caught and sentenced. I hope you've moved on. In fact, I'm counting on that. I need a good man with your legal background and experience, up in the mining district west of Colorado Springs. As you probably know, silver busted in '93, but gold, zinc, coal, and molybdenum are still going strong.

"The fact is, it's not going to be a little man's game much longer. There are some big names surfacing. You ever heard of Winfield Stratton, Spencer Penrose, George Gould, or David Moffat? Them, plus eastern money like the Rockerfellers are moving in. It's causing a ruckus among the small outfits.

"Stratton, for instance, is local—first gold millionaire actually—but the man's peculiar about his money and his holdings. Sold the Independence to a London firm for ten million, still owns other interests there. Workers are beginning to talk union, which is heating things up. I need a man—you—to help the local law keep the peace so production isn't hampered."

Tyler was taking it all in. "So you want me to help the police, sheriff, marshal, or whoever represents the law, right?" Archer nodded. "So then, who's footing the bill? If the townspeople are paying the local law enforcement, then someone else would be paying me."

Archer leaned back in his chair and laced his fingers over his stomach again. "Pinkerton's is your employer. Who pays us is none of your concern at this point. You'll answer to me directly. So are you interested?"

Tyler had a lot to think about. His immediately reaction was to say yes. At over a dollar a day, Chloe's care wasn't going to be cheap, and he had Hank and the new baby to consider, too. Still, he was excited about the prospect of living and working in the Rockies. Raised in Texas, the west had always been in his blood and he realized he missed it.

He stood and gathered up his hat and cane. "I need to talk to my wife. As I told you over the phone, we're moving back here because she's sick. Her health has to be my first concern. Can I get back to you first thing in the morning?"

James Archer swung to his feet and came around the desk. "Perfectly understandable. You and that pretty wife of yours talk it over. I'll even give you an advance on your first month's wages. That should help you get her settled in one of those 'lunger' houses that seem to be sprouting up all over the place."

Tyler bristled at his choice of words. He chose to ignore them. "Thank you, sir. That's very generous of you."

The two shook hands and Tyler made his way to the street, where he caught a trolley that would take him back to the Brown Palace. He stepped off early and walked the last couple of blocks to give himself time to think about all the challenges they were facing. He hated to admit it, but he was scared he would fail and his family would be the ones to suffer.

CHAPTER 35

Auntie Clare and Abel stood on the platform of the Colorado Springs station. Chloe waved from the window of their compartment. "There they are! Oh, let's hurry and get off."

Tyler laughed. "We're ready if you can pull yourself away from the glass."

They traversed the narrow passage, and Tyler helped her down to the platform where she was engulfed in Clare's arms.

"It's our girl, Abel. My, my, we've missed you somethin' terrible." The big woman held her out at arm's length. "And look at you, lookin' like you're carryin' a little, round watermelon under there." She lovingly patted Chloe's belly. "I been a wonderin' when I was gonna get to be a grandma. Them boys of ours certainly don't seem to be in much of a hurry to jump the broom." She turned to where Henry stood looking shy and uneasy. "And you must be Henry. Why, Tyler, I think he looks like you some. Come, give your old grandma a hug."

Chloe could see the boy's hesitation and hoped his qualms were not due to the color of Clare and Abel's skin. She hadn't thought to discuss the fact that they were black folk. They were family. That's all that mattered. She watched his face for his reaction and hoped with all her heart Henry would come to love these two as much as she did. "Henry, I told you all about Auntie Clare and Abel raising me after my mama died. Abel taught me all about nature and Clare taught me how to cook and bake."

Henry looked from Chloe to Tyler and back to the old Negro couple. "Is your apple pie better than ma's? Hers is the best."

Clare bellowed with laughter. "Oh, child, you're a hoot. Course its better. So is my roast, which is what's waitin' in the oven for us back at the house."

Chloe could feel herself relax. She took a deep breath in and smiled. A peace washed over her.

Tyler watched the reunion. His heart rejoiced to see Chloe looking so happy and relaxed. He knew in that moment, this was the right thing for her. Settled into the Morrison's spare rooms, he left to meet with the doctors and the sisters who ran Glockner Sanatorium.

The impressive three-story brick building stood tall with a wing on either side. The design of the new structure was modern and yet had a homey feel about it. People filled the lounging chairs, beds and rockers that occupied the long verandas. Tyler noticed the wide range of ages among the patients, from children to the elderly. He tried hard to overlook the wasted ones who barely left the impression there was a body under the sheets and blankets covering them.

He strolled inside and stood for a moment, taking in his surroundings. *This is nice.* A hand-written sign caught his attention, and he moved closer to read it. In beautiful calligraphy, the notice announced the week's menu. It seemed big meals were served three times a day to entice them to eat and build up their strength. *Hank would probably love eating here.*

"Mr. Reynolds?" Tyler turned to see a handsome woman stride toward him, hand outstretched. "I'm Sister Mary Margaret, Sister Superior for the Sisters of Charity." Tyler's eyebrows came up. She gave a soft chuckle. "I know. That's a lot of sisters in one sentence."

"Sister, I have to admit, I'm pleasantly surprised." He waved a hand at the space around them. "This is better than I'd hoped for. Doctor Brewster said this was one of the most progressive sanatoriums in the country. I'm hoping you're the answer to my prayers."

"We believe God answers prayers in many ways. I hope you're prepared for that."

He followed her to a small office decorated only with a window ledge covered by pots of vivid red geraniums. A simple crucifix hung from one wall while another was graced by a breathtaking view of the mountains. "Glockner's is certainly situated in a beautiful spot."

"Yes, the sanatorium was founded in 1890 by a young widow, Marie Gwynne Glockner, as a memorial to her husband. It was given over to the Sisters of Charity of Cincinnati in 1893. I've been blessed to have been brought in as Sister Superior of Nurses last year."

She picked up a file from the corner of her desk. "Let's take care of business, and then I'll turn you over to Sister Rosemary. She's the charge nurse over the women's wing."

Dressed entirely in white, Sister Rosemary walked sedately beside Tyler, her hands clasped in front of her. "You're in luck, Mr. Reynolds. Your wife's room has an excellent view of the mountains and being on the end, it's quiet. I know you requested private quarters, but that's just not possible with the influx of guests we are seeing. Every one of our private huts is occupied. We even have waiting lists for outside beds. I understand a letter from Mr. Roosevelt moved your wife to the top of the list for a semi-private room."

Tyler was shocked, unaware TR had intervened on Chloe's behalf. He had no idea the demand for space was so high. A moment of guilt bubbled up and vanished almost as quickly as it came. He didn't care if Chloe was taking someone else spot as long as it meant she would be cured. *I'll have to thank him.*

"I've placed Mrs. Reynolds in a room with a sweet woman from Georgia named Laura Lee Wilcox. She'll be wonderful company for your wife."

Tyler smiled down at the kindly woman. "Thank you, Sister. As I told Sister Mary Margaret, I think your place here has been an answer to our prayers. I'll be bringing my wife over tomorrow to get her settled in and I plan to find a home close by for my son and I."

Tyler left the facility feeling more confident about Chloe's care going forward. The one thing he dreaded telling her was that she wouldn't be able to have the baby stay with her once she delivered. *We'll cross that bridge when we come to it.*

He returned to the Morrison's pretty little bungalow to find Henry exploring the yard with Abel. Chloe and Clare were in the kitchen having a high old time making cookies. He snatched one off the cooling rack. "Mm, snickerdoodles, my favorite." He studied Chloe. The hollowness in her cheeks and the smudges under her eyes contradicted her standard statement of 'I'm fine'. "Darling, have you rested since we got here?"

Chloe sighed, causing the scarf over her mouth and nose to flutter. The smile he couldn't see on her lips shined in her eyes. "No, I've been enjoying myself too much. I suppose you're going to make me go lie down, aren't you?"

Tyler pulled her to her feet and gently rubbed a thumb under her eye. "These dark circles are telling on you. Why don't you go rest? You'll have all the time in the world to be with Clare and Abel. Now scoot off to bed." He gave her backside a playful swat. As soon as she left the room, he dropped into the chair she'd occupied and swiped a palm across his brow.

Clare wiped her hands on her apron, lowered herself onto the bench across from him, and laid her hand on his arm. "Talk to me, son. That wasn't the Chloe we know who just walked out of here, besides the fact that she actually left without a fight, that girl's skin and bone."

Tyler gathered her pudgy hands in his. "Coming here has got to work, Clare. I can't lose her."

"I've been prayin' every hour, every day since you called, so has Abel. You have to be strong and trust in the Great Physician, son." She gave his hands a squeeze. "Now what can we do to help?"

Relief washed over him. To share the burden took a great weight off his shoulders. "I'm taking her to the Glockner Sanatorium in the morning. They'll be taking care of her. Once I get her settled, I need to head up to Cripple Creek." He hesitated to make his next request. It was a lot to ask. "I was hoping Hank could stay here with you. I assume school's still in session. Once he's enrolled, he'll be out of your hair most of the day, and I should be back in ten days. Then I'll look for a house for the two of us."

Clare hoisted her large frame up away from the table. "Don't you worry about a thing. And while you're up there at the mines, look my boys up. They got themselves a claim called 'The Lucky Lady'."

"Clare, there's something else you should know. She can't keep the baby with her once it comes." He bowed his head and let out a tired sigh. "I haven't had the heart or the courage to tell her yet."

Tyler watched Clare pull a sheet of cookies out of the oven and settle them on a rack. Her face scrunched up at the news, and then, as if she knew the outcome, she planted her hands on her ample hips and shrugged. "Well, we have us a good two-and-a-half months for the Lord to work that out."

CHAPTER 36

Chloe stepped to the large open window that occupied most of one wall. A sweet breeze lifted the light, gauzy curtains. The view was beautiful, with tall, rugged pine-covered peaks in the distance and a meadow of wildflowers at their base. "It's lovely."

She turned back to smile at the youngish nurse who was folding down the bedding. She had startling blue eyes framed by dark eyebrows. Chloe imagined her hair was black like her own under the long wimple that graced her head and surrounded her pleasant face. "I'm sure I'll be very happy here. Tell me, do you have a library?"

"Oh, yes, Mrs. Reynolds, a very extensive one was donated to us by Mr. and Mrs. Penrose. We encourage our guests to read to themselves or those that can't while taking in the sun."

"Please call me Chloe. I'm a journalist and photographer. Would it be okay if I interview other patients and take pictures?"

The nurse pursed her lips and scrunched her dark eyebrows. "Please call them guests, not patients. I think you'll have to speak to Sister Mary Margaret about the writing and photos. We have to consider everyone's privacy, you know. Now here is your first dose of medication. You'll receive it four times a day throughout your stay here as well as three healthy meals." She picked up a sheet of paper on the stand between the beds. "Here's our daily schedule. Please familiarize yourself with it so you'll know what to expect. It also lists the rules we require our guests to follow."

Chloe took the glass and looked at the brown concoction. "What is it?" A whiff made her jerk away and make a face. "It smells awful."

"It's a special mix of herbs Dr. Ambrose has found to help build up the immune system and relieve the symptoms of consumption. It's quite effective." She smiled. "As for the taste and smell, we're working on that."

Chloe took a deep breath and gulped down the brew. "It's not as bad as I thought it would be." She tried hard not to make a face and wondered how she would get through four of those a day.

"I'll leave you now. My name is Sister Prudence. I'll be one of your primary caregivers so we'll get to know each other well, I'm sure. The woman you'll be sharing the room with, Laura Lee, is out on the veranda taking in her required four hours of morning sun. Once you feel settled, I suggested you go on out and join her and the others. You'll be expected to spend the bulk of your time out of doors."

Chloe waited for the nun to leave before she reached for the pitcher of water on the bedside table. "That's was some nasty stuff." She made a face.

With the new fountain pen Tyler had given her and notebook in hand, she wandered outside. The new notebook was to record her thoughts and observations with the idea of writing an article someday. With one in seven Americans contracting TB, Chloe was sure people would be interested to know what it was like on the inside of a sanatorium.

Intending to find a secluded rocker overlooking the expansive herb and flower garden, Chloe stepped outside. She was shocked to see twenty or so women occupying a long row of beds that lined the veranda. Others sat in rockers or lounged in deck chairs. Many of their faces told their story. Dark hollows and sunken eyes emphasized the wasting disease that was eating them alive. Several smiled at her and motioned her over. Suddenly shy and uncomfortable, she headed down the path and found a stone bench among the flowers instead.

The beauty that surrounded her did little to dispel her somber mood. *Will I look like that in a few months?* A new thought crowded in. One she'd been keeping at bay since the day they got the devastating news. *Lord, will my baby even have a chance to know her mama?*

Tears broke free at a loss she was only beginning to feel. She already missed Tyler and Hank, not to mention Auntie Clare and Abel. With a cough and an intake of sweet mountain air, she lifted her chin in stubborn defiance. "We're in this together, baby girl." She rubbed circles over her stomach and closed her eyes. "I won't give up, I promise."

❦

Tyler stepped down from the train and made his way into the station. It was a busier place than he had anticipated. Folks of every ilk moved in and out of the building. A colorful parrot squawked from his perch. "Burn out! Burn out!"

Tyler flipped a coin to a newsboy. "What's that bird talking about?"

The kid waved a hand at the exotic bird. "Aw, that's all he says since the fire burned the town down a coupla years back. I think the smoke made him crazy."

Tyler tucked the paper under one arm and gave the big-beaked bird a wide berth. It had been a year since his last visit here with Roosevelt. If anything, the town seemed bigger and busier. "Which way to the National Hotel?"

"Straight up Bennett past the Machine Works."

Cripple Creek stepped up the hillside in a mix of brick buildings and clapboard houses with nary a tree in sight. Tyler couldn't see a lot of difference between it and Victor. Several colossal mine temples dotted the landscape, surrounded by slag heaps of discarded waste ore that stained the surrounding slopes rusty.

Although he didn't need his cane for support anymore, it had become a habit to carry it. Now he used it to catch the door before it shut as a couple came out of the hotel. Tyler stepped inside and surveyed the interior. The lobby was making a nice try at opulence and succeeding. Although Tyler been here before, the crowds had kept him from noticing. Pleased, Tyler made his way to the counter. "Mr. Reynolds. I believe you have a room reserved for me."

The young clerk smiled a greeting and ran his finger down a list. "Yes, sir. Room two twelve." He handed him a key and an envelope. "This was waiting for you, sir."

Tyler stepped away and opened the envelope to find a single slip of paper inside.

Meeting set with Marshal Boyd
and mine representatives
10am Court House, Bennett Ave.
Cripple Creek

FRAGILE REPRIEVE

Keep quiet and listen.
Expect report upon return
James Archer

He pocketed the note and carried his valise to his room. Nervous energy coursed through him—something he hadn't felt since his outlaw days riding with the Wild Bunch. *Keep a handle on it, Reynolds. Don't forget who you are this time.*

❧

The morning broke crisp and clear, promising a beautiful day. Already on Cripple Creek's main road, Tyler headed up Bennett Avenue, passed the jail to the Teller County Court House. He stepped inside and removed his hat, giving himself time to let his eyes adjust.

A thin, severe-looking woman eyed him over the small, round glasses perched on her pointy nose. "May I help you?"

Tyler moved to the counter and gave her his best smile. "Yes, ma'am. Thank you. I have a meeting with Marshal Boyd and some gentlemen."

She gave him a critical once over and crooked a finger, apparently deeming him satisfactory. "Follow me."

The room they entered was lavishly appointed. The five men occupying the club chairs that flanked a large stone fireplace stood when he entered. *Here goes nothing.* Tyler squared his shoulders, stepped forward, and extended his hand to the first man. "Tyler Reynolds, Pinkerton National Detective Agency."

Tall and broad-shouldered, the big man gripped his hand so hard Tyler fought to keep the wince from his face and continued to smile. "Nathaniel Boyd. I'm the law in these parts." He adjusted his gun belt as if to affirm his authority. His steely look never wavered.

He doesn't like having me here. Best keep on his good side.

A smaller, foppishly dressed man stepped up. His palm was moist in Tyler's. "Timothy Teasdale, representing Venture Corporation and Stratton's Limited of London. We have several interests in the District. I was the one who convinced these gentlemen we needed outside assistance. Hope you don't prove me wrong."

"I'll do everything I can to see that things remain on an even keel. Pinkerton's is ready to send more men should the need arise."

At six feet, the next man stood eye level to Tyler, but outweighed him by thirty pounds. The gray hair and handlebar mustache matched his cold gray eyes. "Sean Corrigan, manager of the Portland." He pointed to the two remaining men. "This is Charles McCormick from the Vindicator and Russell Stokes who manages the Dolly Mae."

Mr. Teasdale motioned to the chairs. "Gentlemen, let's get down to business, shall we?"

Almost an hour later, Tyler was back in his room, undoing his string tie and loosening his tight collar. Whatever he had expected from the meeting, he knew one thing for sure, these men were playing for keeps. Millions in gold was at stake and they meant to have it.

He still wasn't completely sure how his presence in the District was going to make a big difference or what exactly his job would be. He was to report to the Portland manager's office in Victor first thing in the morning for a tour and an explanation of his duties.

That gave Tyler the afternoon to learn the layout of
Cripple Creek and the surrounding camps that made up the
district. It also gave him time to see if he could locate
Matthew and John Morrison. He'd promised Clare and
Abel he would look them up and deliver a tin of cookies
from their mama.

He changed from his suit to western garb. "Now that's
better." He had forgotten how comfortable the soft feel of
cotton and denim were. From his valise, Tyler pulled out
his holster and gun. It was the same one he carried when
running with Butch Cassidy and Sundance—the one his
father tried to protect his mother with. As good as it felt on
his hip, he hoped he would never have cause to use it.
Donning his new tan Stetson and leaving his cane behind,
he headed out to explore the town. After a hearty meal, he
found the livery and hired a horse for the duration of his
stay.

"You ride much?" asked the grizzled old man who
saddled up the bay gelding for him.

"Not in a while." He climbed up into the saddle and
reached down to adjust the stirrups to match his long legs.
"This critter got a name?"

"Name is Moses after my granddaddy 'cause he pushes
through and don't give up."

The horse proved to be sure-footed but a plodder, not
like the roan he used to ride. The two spent the afternoon
moving over the pockmarked landscape that marred the
mountainsides surrounding the camps. At one mine, he
found an old codger who reminded him of Jasper Johnson.
Gray bristle covered the old man's craggy face and a dirty
sweat-stained rag of a hat perched on his head. "Howdy.
Strike it big yet?"

The old prospector ambled up and shaded his eyes with a work-worn hand while the other cradled a Winchester. "Who you be, sonny boy? Don't like no strangers gettin' any ideas about jumpin' my claim."

Tyler stayed in the saddle and rested an arm across the horn. "I'm looking for the Lucky Lady. You heard tell of it?"

Without shifting his stance, the miner pointed off to the south. "Couple of darkies workin' a claim called the Lucky Lady over on the back side of Battle Mountain above Victor. Ain't heard if they're pulling out any good yella color yet." He turned and stomped off toward the yawning mouth of the mineshaft. "Can't be jawin' all day. Gold's a'comin', I can smell it." Without so much as a backward glance, the man disappeared into the cave.

Tyler reined Moses to the south and worked his way across the hillside camps of Anaconda and Elkton. An hour later, he found what he was looking for. Climbing down from the saddle, he stretched his back. Off to one side, a flat section had been leveled off. A canvas tent occupied the space and was fronted by a ring of stones surrounding cold ashes.

The only greeting he got was from an Appaloosa that whinnied from an aspen-railed corral. Tyler hiked up the crooked path to the equally crooked opening that yawned out of the steep slope. A hand-painted sign announced to the world that the Lucky Lady was owned and operated by the Morrison Brothers. Below this, it warned that anyone caught trespassing would be shot first and identified later. Tyler chuckled. Identified had an extra 't' in it.

He stepped into the cool gloom of the mine and cased his hands around his mouth. "Hello in there." His voice echoed and bounced off the rough surface of the walls.

There was no answer except for the distant sound of a pick against rock deep in the bowels of the mine. "This is not my idea of fun." Tyler muttered to himself as he moved further into the dark recesses. He glanced over his shoulder to assure himself the opening was within view. "Matt? John? It's Tyler Reynolds. You guys in here?"

The ping of steel striking stone stopped. *Good, they must have heard me.* The dank, flat darkness giving him the creeps, Tyler quickly moved back up the sloping floor toward the sunlight. *I don't know how anyone could spend hours and hours down in those holes.* He found a place on a large boulder warmed by the sun and waited.

A good ten minutes passed before the brothers came through the entrance. Already dark-skinned, the grim and dirt made them appear even blacker. The whites of their eyes and teeth flashed when they saw Tyler perched on the rock near the mouth of the mine.

John slapped his brother's shoulder. "You owe me two bits. I told you it sounded like Chloe's husband."

Matt flicked off the oil feed to the lamp attached to his leather cap and pulled the whole thing off, causing a wealth of springy black hair to come alive. "Good to see you again."

Tyler stood and met the two men halfway. "I'd shake your hands, but I'm not sure the hotel has enough water to clean me up afterwards. Looks like awfully dirty work."

"Always liked playing in the dirt," laughed John. "Good to see ya."

The brothers went to a bucket and started cleaning up. "Ma said you were bringing Chloe out here for treatment. How is she?" Matt asked.

"If you want to know the truth, I'm scared for her. Having consumption is bad enough, but being pregnant on top of that." Tyler shook his head and ran a hand through his hair. "I got her settled in at Glockner Sanatorium. It seems like a good place and came highly recommended."

"Squirt's a fighter." Washed up, John shook Tyler's hand, then planted himself on an adjacent rock. "She won't give up and neither should you."

Matt clapped his hands. "We've got to go into the Springs in a couple of days. We'll go see her. That should brighten her day."

Tyler dusted his hat against his outstretched leg. "Not sure they'll let you, with their rules and all. I guess it's worth a try. She could use some cheering up. Right now, she's feeling like a pariah. People see the scarf she wears over her mouth and they back away. The whole country is terrified of catching TB."

"You can't blame them. It's killing people by the thousands. Alaska has some of the highest death rates around." Matt moved back inside the mine entrance and came out with a burlap bag. "This is why we're headed into the Springs."

Tyler took the heavy gunnysack and opened the top. He drew out a large chuck of rock. The sun glinted off the grayish-white surface as Tyler turned it over in his hands. It was streaked on all sides with bright color. "Is this what I think it is?"

"Yep, that's called sylvanite telluride. That bag is full of samples. John and I have been digging like a couple of moles for months. We're down a good hundred feet. Ran into some water in the cross cut so decided to head off in a different direction. That drift has a good, strong vein. I think we've only hit the beginning of it."

John reached down and picked up a similar size rock from the slag at his feet. "This stuff's worthless, but that, my friend, is gonna make us rich." He swung back and pitched the waste rock down the mountainside. "Matt and I don't trust the assayers around here. They're likely in the big man's pocket along with the law. That's why we're headed into the city."

Tyler's detective instincts kicked in. "How do you know that? What kind of evidence do you have that's what's going on?"

Matt snorted. "Ain't no proof except every time a small outfit like ours gets a strike, the assayers claim it ain't gonna amount to nothing. They convince the miner he should sale now and at least get something for it. Then the big boys swoop in and buy them out. If the little guy won't budge, he's threatened with a lawsuit. The big outfits will buy up the claims around it for next to nothing.

"Ya see, if the vein comes out to the surface on someone else's claim, your whole vein could be theirs. It's called the law of apex. Horizontal veins like ours can run a long way before surfacing. We need to figure out where the updrift is and if it's still on our claim before word gets out."

John tag-teamed in. "Yeah, we've seen it happen a half dozen times since we've been here. Biggest example is the Portland. These two Irish guys had themselves a tiny little sliver of land, hit a horizontal vein. Almost blew it, but they teamed up with Old Man Stratton himself, and the rest is history. They quietly bought up claim after claim and that little strip of land turned into a hundred and eighty some acres. Now they're the big boys.

"Working the Klondike was rough. There your biggest adversaries are the elements. If you're a hard-rock miner down here, nobody pays you no never-mind until you strike a vein. An especially a big one like this—suddenly you got to watch your back. If the little guy won't budge, pretty soon strange things start to happen and he's forced to make a deal or lose everything."

Matt held the sack out for Tyler to drop the sample back in. "If you're lucky, you might end up with a quarter of what your claim is really worth. Crazy Bob Womack had a million dollar strike, and he's walking around penniless now. If we can find someone to give us a grubstake, this will be our ticket to the good life. We don't aim to break our backs to make some other bugger richer."

The men gave Tyler a lot to think about. Maybe he was on the wrong side of the fence. He wasn't about to be a strong arm for greedy profiteers.

Easing up from the boulder, he settled his hat back on his head. "Come on up to Cripple Creek tonight and I'll buy you dinner. I'm staying at the National." He mounted his horse and started to turn away. "Oh, I almost forgot." He reached into the saddlebag draped across the bay's haunches and pulled out the round tin. "These are from your mother." He tossed the container to John. "Snickerdoodles. Might be one or two missing." Tyler grinned and dug his heels into Mose's soft underbelly to spur him forward.

"See ya tonight. I'll be having myself a thick slab of steak since you're buying," John shouted after him.

CHAPTER 37

Tyler followed Corrigan through the first office. The big man was in his element and trying to impress by spouting off about mining techniques and using terms Tyler was sure not to know. They stopped next to a large piece of machinery.

Corrigan pointed at the huge cogged iron wheels. "This here's a Webster, Camp, and Lane first motion hoist." He switched directions. "Over there is a bank of dynamos capable of powering eight hundred lights. We have three main shafts. This one is the Burns Shaft, named after James Burns, the original partner and president of Portland Gold Mining Company." He stepped to a metal cage. "You ready to go down?"

This was the moment Tyler dreaded. The thought of going deep into the recesses of the mountain made him break out in a sweat. Corrigan gave him a challenging smirk. "Not squeamish, are you?"

Tyler grabbed a cap and oil wick can off the shelf next to the cage. "Can't wait." The wire cage carried them down a lot faster than he expected. "How far are we going?" He yelled into Corrigan's ear.

"This one goes a thousand feet, but we're going to stop at the Number Two."

The cage came to a grinding halt. Tyler followed the mine manager out into a large timber-framed space.

"This is the seven-hundred foot station. Over there is the Number Two, and that way is the Anna Lee. We got lucky with that one—had a shaft collapse in ninety-six killing eight men. When we were cutting the drift to get to the bodies, we uncovered several more rich veins."

"Lucky? I bet those men didn't think so."

Corrigan shrugged his indifference. "That's the chance you take working underground. Besides, Burns and Stratton paid off the families so they aren't hurting none."

Tyler couldn't believe the manager's lack of empathy or compassion. If he was like that about his own men, he could only imagine what he was like with competitors. "I think I've seen enough. I'm ready to go back up."

Corrigan sneered. "Guess it's a good thing you'll be doing your spying topside. It takes a certain kind of man to work underground, someone who ain't afraid of Tommyknockers."

Tyler refused to take the bait and ask what a Tommyknocker was. To keep his temper in check, he took a few slow breaths in and out. He and the mine manager weren't going to be friends—that was obvious—but he still had to work with the man, so he needed to keep it civil. They climbed back into the cage and headed to the top. His body relaxed the closer they got to the surface. "Anything else I should see?"

"Just the changing rooms. Put them up to stop the high-grading that was going on."

Tyler didn't want to ask, and waited for Corrigan to explain. They stepped into a good-sized room. Clothes hung from hooks on all four walls. Benches took up the middle space. The large sign on the opposite wall answered his question. In big, black letters it read:

HIGH GRADING WILL NOT BE TOLERATED!
Any Portland employee caught stealing ore in any amount,
will be fired immediately and prosecuted.

Corrigan pointed to the sign. "If it were up to me,
they'd be shot."

Tyler left the Portland, mounted Moses, and headed
back to Cripple Creek where he waited for Matt and John
to show up. When it had been dark for almost an hour, he
decided to eat without them and assumed they changed
their minds. *Their loss.*

He eyed the slab of beef the waitress put before
him. The twelve-ounce steak was cooked to perfection, as
were the new potatoes and asparagus. With no room for
dessert, he headed back to his room, saddle-sore and tired.

❧

The next morning he made the seven-mile trip south to
Victor and tied up in front of the post office. The man
behind the counter waved a hand. "Howdy. What can I do
for ya?"

Tyler stepped up and extended a hand. "Mr. Sullivan,
you probably don't remember me. I was here about a year
ago with Vice President Roosevelt's campaign tour. I
wanted to stop by and thank you once again for your quick
thinking that day. If you hadn't stepped in and kept that
man from swinging that post, Mr. Roosevelt might never
have made it to the White House."

"Well, all be darn, I remember you. Call me Danny.
Mr. Sullivan is my father." Daniel Sullivan jumped over
the counter and pumped Tyler's hand up and down. "What
brings you back to Victor?"

"I'm visiting a couple of friends. You know Matt and John Morrison over at the Lucky Lady?"

Sullivan chuckled. "There are hundreds of want-a-be miners claiming chunks of these mountains and more arriving daily. Can't say I've heard of them. Where are they digging?"

"Up on the northwest face of Battle Mountain passed the Ajax."

"That's over toward Elkton. I have to make a delivery up there. If you're headed that way, I'll ride along and keep you company."

Tyler waited while the postmaster locked up and, side by side, they rode out. When they came on to the Morrison claim, they were met by an eerie quiet. The canvas tent the brothers lived in lay collapsed on one end. Supplies were strewn haphazardly around the site. The two burros and both horses Tyler had seen in the makeshift corral the day before were gone. "Something doesn't feel right."

CHAPTER 38

His instincts on high alert, Tyler drew his gun and swung down off his horse. Danny joined him, pulling a Winchester from the scabbard attached to his saddle. "Maybe they ran out of liquor and headed down to town last night."

Tyler shook his head. "They don't drink and this place didn't look like this yesterday. Let's check out the mine." He moved into the entrance and grabbed a lantern. A match to the wick illuminated the dark cavern in front of them. Together they hiked deeper down the slope into the bowels of the mine until they came to a windlass on a hoist over a three-foot wide hole. The horizontal tunnel ended a few feet past the abyss.

Tyler kneeled, held the lantern over the shaft, and hollered. "Hello, anyone down there? Matt… John?" He listened intently. "Did you hear that?"

Danny got down beside him. His ear turned to the opening. "Sounds like somebody's down there."

They strained to pick up any sound. "There! It sounded like someone was calling for help." Tyler pressed up and holstered his gun. He handed Sullivan the lantern and swung around to lower himself into the hole. His feet feeling for the rungs of the homemade ladder, he eased down until only his head remained above the hole's edge.

"Hand me the light, then go see if you can find another one. I'll wait for you at the bottom."

Tyler worked his way down the ladder. After what he guessed was about fifteen feet, he reached the dirt floor. Swinging the lantern around in front of him, he could see another shaft angling downward a few feet away. The amount of work the two men had done was impressive. "Matthew and John Morrison, are you down here?" he shouted.

Far away, he thought he heard someone holler back. Encouraged, he looked up the passage. Sullivan was working his way down, a lantern swinging from his hand. "Hurry up, I think I hear them."

A minute later, Sullivan jumped to the ground. "I grabbed a rope just in case. Could you tell where their voices were coming from?"

"No, but they're in trouble. Let's go."

The two men maneuvered down the narrow slope until it divided into two more shafts.

"Which one do we take?" Sullivan asked.

"I'll take the left, you take the right, if it goes more than twenty feet come back and get me, I'll do the same." Each man took off. Tyler quickly came to the end of his tunnel and headed back to see what Danny had found. The man was kneeling next to another hole. "The ladder's all busted up over there." Tyler got down on his knees and cupped his hands around his mouth. "Matt... John, can you hear me?"

What Tyler thought was John's voice floated up to them. "Tyler, is that you? We're down here. Matt's hurt. We're standing in water up to our chests and it's getting deeper."

"Hold on, we're coming." Tyler turned to Sullivan. "We need to tie off that rope and you can lower me down."

They found a solid up-thrust of rock and worked the rope around it. Danny braced his legs against the base and leaned back. Tyler tied the other end around his waist, leaving enough to tie the lantern to the end. "Ready?"

"Yep." Sullivan nodded.

Tyler eased over the lip. "Go slow until I know what I'm dropping into." After a couple of feet, the chimney gave way to a cavern with steeply sloped sides. "Lower me down." He swung free and twisted around. His boots touched water. The flickering light showed him a room the size of a small bedroom. John had Matt laying up against him half in and half out of the water. "Is he conscious?"

"He's been in and out." John hoisted his brother a little higher. "We were ambushed. I think there were three of them. They were waiting at the first hole and whacked us each good as we climbed out. Next thing I know, I'm waking up in here. Thank God, you came back."

Tyler undid the lantern and dropped into the pool. The shock made him suck in his breath. "This is like ice water!"

"We think we hit a small natural spring. Yesterday it was only to our ankles, now it's up past my waist and rising."

Tyler untied himself and plowed through the frigid water to John's side. "Here, hold this and let me have him." He handed off their only source of light and stooped, chin deep to get a hold of one of Matt's arms and a leg. With a mighty bellow, he strained to hoist Matt's limp body over his shoulder. Freezing water poured from the man's clothes down Tyler's face, causing him to sputter and gasp. He struggled to where the rope hung. "I need you to come help me get this rope around under his arms."

John swam over. His jaw tensed, and his eyes closed for a second. Tyler could see the pain etched on his face. "What's the matter? You hurt too?"

"I think I broke my foot when they threw us in here. We can't worry about that now. We've got to get Matt out of here. I hope you brought a lot of help."

Tyler snorted. "I didn't know I was going to need to rescue your butts. Danny Sullivan, the postmaster, is up top. That's it."

"I guess we're on our own then."

Together the two men worked the loop around Matt's feet and up over his waist to his broad chest. He mumbled something and started trashing around. John grabbed his brother's face between his palms. "Matt, wake up. We're getting out of here." He gave him a gently slap. "Come on, wake up."

Matt's eyes fluttered open. "What happened?" He started to twist and struggle.

"Whoa." Tyler clamped his arms around the man's legs. "We're going to get you out of here, but you've got to hold still." Matt complied by passing out. Tyler raised his face toward the opening. "Danny, can you pull him up?"

Matt was a good size man, every bit as big as Daniel Sullivan. Tyler heaved up with everything in him. John did the same. Between their combined efforts, they managed to move him a couple of feet.

Sullivan shouted down. "It's no use. I can't get any leverage. I'm easing him back down. We're gonna have to think of something else."

Tyler took Matt's weight and lowered him into the water. He rubbed a hand across his forehead. *God, help me. I need to think.* He looked at John. "Do you have another ladder somewhere? We found the one that you must have made for this hole. It's hacked up into several sections."

"We only have the two. I think the first one will be long enough if your friend can get it down here. There are a couple of places that might be troublesome."

Tyler hollered up to Danny. "Did you hear that? John thinks the first ladder might work."

"Hold tight, I'll go get it."

John huffed. "Like we're going someplace."

It seemed to take forever before they heard Danny again. Tyler stood directly beneath the opening and held the lantern up to see Sullivan's face staring down at him over the edge. "Well? Tyler asked.

Danny frowned and shook his head. "It's a no go. There wasn't enough room to get it around one of the bends. I think I'd better go get help. I can be back with a crew in under an hour."

Tyler looked at Matt. He didn't know how to judge a black man's color, but he didn't look good. "Go. And Sullivan, move fast."

CHAPTER 39

For the three trapped men, time passed excruciatingly slow. At least Tyler thought so. "How do you stand working down here for hours on end? I'd go crazy."

John adjusted his brother's head where is rested on his shoulder. "Most miners will tell you, we're all one nugget shy of the mother-lode. It's not so bad if you know you can get to the surface."

"Which I hope we can do soon, I'm beginning to lose the feeling in my toes."

"What toes?" John scoffed. "At least the cold water is helping with the pain in my foot."

"Shh… I hear something!" Tyler waded to the opening and strained to listen. "Hello! Anybody there?"

A lantern appeared, followed by Danny's face and several other men. "Zek here had a bigger windlass at his claim. We're rigging it up now. Should be able to haul you all up out of there in a minute. I'm sending down a harness."

Tyler caught the contraption attached to a stout rope and maneuvered the leather straps around Matt's legs and chest and buckled him in. "Matt, hold on, buddy, we're getting you out of here. Okay, haul him up."

Tyler and John watched Matt make the slow ascent until he disappeared through the narrow chimney. Tyler smiled at John and slapped him on the back. "You're next."

John gave him a crooked smile. "Thanks for coming back. We'd have died down here if it weren't for you. We owe ya."

Embarrassed, Tyler grabbed the dangling harness as it dropped back down the shaft and shoved it at him. "Quit jawin' and get up there so I can get out of here. You may not mind these dark holes, but they give me the creeps."

Everyone topside, a couple of the rescuers grumbled and spat wads of slimy black tobacco when they saw the color of Matt and John's skin. "Don't know what we're wastin' our time here for" they mumbled a few derogatory names and walked away. The brothers ignored them as if they were used to that kind of treatment. Tyler took his cue for them and headed to the partially collapsed tent to change out of his wet clothes.

Matt came around enough to dress himself and complain about his head hurting. "I'd like to get my hands on whoever it was who clocked us and stole our samples?"

One of the men introduced himself. "Zek Baker, up over yonder at the Rosa Mae. I ain't had much doings with black folk like yourselves, but a miner is a miner and a claim's a claim in my book. It's making me plumb cantankerous having to look over my shoulder constantly. Why I've taken to carrying a pick in one hand and a shotgun in the other and that don't allow for gettin' much work done. This here's the fourth claim that's had some kind of theft. How many thievin' skunks you think there were?"

John shook his head and shrugged. "Hard to say. They caught us by surprised and hit us both over the head before we even knew what was happening."

Danny played doctor and examined Matt's head. "You could probably use some stitches. You got a lump the size of a turkey egg going on back here."

"It'll take more than a tap on the noggin to do the Morrison boys in." Matt snorted, then winced at Danny's touch.

Another man, bow-legged and leather-faced, chimed in. "It's one thing high gradin' them big outfits like the Independence or Portland. They have more waste ore than we can dig." He spat a stream of tobacco and covered a wild daisy in black gunk. "To rob from a fella digger is just plain wrong." He took off a dirty, stained hat and slapped it across his leg. "Why, they'd have to shoot me before they got their measly hands on any of my ore."

Heads nodded all around.

Tyler sat back and listened to the men voice their concerns about the attack and theft. Whoever the perpetrators were, resorting to deadly force to get what they wanted told him these men weren't afraid of the law in these parts or were too reckless to care. Tyler thought back to meeting Marshal Boyd. The man was a freight train with legs and looked like he meant business. Anyone with any smarts would know better than to tangle with him, which brought up another question. If they didn't have any reason to be afraid, then who's pocket was Boyd in?

CHAPTER 40

Eyes closed and head laid back, Chloe smiled at the warm feel of the sun against her skin. She'd been at the sanatorium for six days and she felt better already. Her skin went from a pale, grayish pallor to a warm, sun kissed glow. The cough hadn't diminished, nor had the fatigue, but she was hopeful that would come with time.

Sister Prudence was a delight. She never seemed to have a cross word, or mind working with the contagious guests. As much as Chloe liked her and appreciated her kindness, she didn't make up for not being allowed visitors.

Laura Lee, the woman she shared the room with, was the one who informed her no visitors were allowed. The blond, blue-eyed Georgia woman was thirty-three, although she looked years older. She was probably comely before the consumption got her. Now her hair was thin and dull, her skin sallow, and her eyes held a haunted, wistful look.

"There's something about ya all that I can't put my finger on." Laura Lee tilled her head and searched Chloe's face. "I think you're going to make it out of here. You *and* your baby."

Chloe felt hope rise at her words. If Laura Lee could see it, surely it was more than her own wishful thinking. "I've been doing a lot of praying. I just hope God's listening."

"Oh, he's listening." Laura Lee nodded. "Sometimes we just don't like his answer. Me, I've lived a good life and I've been blessed. Even in those moments when I thought I'd been abandoned, he was there if I had taken the time to look."

"You sound like Auntie Clare. She would say you can't see the blessings if you don't look up."

Laura Lee laid her head back against the pillow and closed her eyes. "I've been doing a lot of looking up lying in this bed. You know at first I was so angry with God I could have spit in his eye and believe me, proper southern ladies do not spit.

"Then over the past eleven months I've been here, I've changed. Having so much time on my hands has afforded me the opportunity to look back at my life and appreciate every moment, even the bad ones." She struggled to prop herself up on one elbow. "Of course I have regrets, we all do, but even my mistakes have made me who I am today, and that's something to be proud of.

"Chloe, I'm not likely to make it out of here."

"Oh, Laura Lee, don't say that."

Laura Lee waved her protests away. "It's okay, sweety. There's more than one way to get well. When you leave here, I want you to do something for me—for all of us. You need to tell our story. Take my picture and put it side by side next to the one in that case in my bureau drawer so folks can see what this terrible disease does to people. We're lucky to be in a decent, caring place like this but so many aren't as fortunate. You have the talent and power to tell the world and make them listen."

Tears filled Chloe's eyes and fragmented the scene before her until she blinked them away. She reached over from the rocking chair she'd pulled up next to the bed and touched Laura Lee's arm. "We're both going to get out of here and you can help me write the story."

Laura Lee smiled. "Sounds like a plan, but just in case, my diary's in the same drawer, I want you to have it." She coughed up a bloody mass and spat it into a cup. Chloe looked away, the sight making her nauseous. Laura Lee's eyes closed, and she breathed a weary sigh. "So tired…"

Chloe eased out of the rocker and tiptoed back inside to collect her own journal and a pen. The clock on the wall said she had thirty minutes before she would be expected in the dining hall. Enough time to record her thoughts and Laura Lee's wise words.

She made her way down the stone walkway to her favorite bench in the garden. The short distance was exhausting and several times, she had to stop as ragged coughing doubled her over. She inspected the hankie in her hand for signs of blood. Relief washed over her when it still appeared clean. Once settle on the bench, she took the time to close her eyes and breathe in the lovely fragrance of lavender, rose, and lilac. The heady perfume never ceased to calm her and fill her with peace.

Chloe opened her book and flipped to the next blank page. Her pen poised, she thought about what Laura Lee said and looked at her own life. She had been so blessed, even in the dark moments like when her mother died. Auntie Clare was right there to love and nurture her, and after her father died, God gave her Tyler. She couldn't imagine her life without him. "I miss you so much, my love," she whispered, envisioning her words being carried to him on the breeze.

Chloe sat and wrote. The words came of their own volition and flowed across the pages. A hand on her shoulder startled her and brought her back to the present.

"It's time to go in for supper." Sister Prudence smiled down at her. "I'll walk back with you."

Chloe looked up at the nurse and wondered what made her risk her own health to care for others. *I need to get her story someday.* Her eyes scanned the tall building. *I need to get all their stories.* With a new purpose, Chloe linked her arm in the Sister's. Together, patient and nurse, they followed the path to the central hall where the other ambulatory guests were being served a nutritious meal.

Never a big eater, Chloe cleaned her plate and drink a full glass of milk while having polite conservation with the people at her table. They were from all walks of life—an opera singer, a farmer, a traveling preacher, a grandmother, a stagecoach driver. It seemed no one was immune to the White Plague.

With a forced smile, she downed her prescribed dose of the herbal concoction. *If it makes me well, I'd drink a gallon a day.* Still, she couldn't help the shutter that traveled down her body at the nasty taste. Similar expressions crossed everyone else's face as they took their medicine before leaving the table.

Pleased with herself and determined to be more thoughtful of the people around her, Chloe volunteered to carry a tray back to Laura Lee's bedside on the veranda. The bed was empty, a speckled splatter of blood bright against the pillow. Chloe turned and hurried to their shared room.

The beds were made, the room undisturbed. She sat the tray down. *Where could she be?*

Anxious dread propelled Chloe down the hall. Sister Mary Margaret and Dr. Ambrose stepped out of a room, their faces somber. The head nurse saw Chloe first and mustered a smile that never quite made it to her eyes. "Mrs.

Reynolds, I'm afraid we have some sad news." She reached out and gently gathered Chloe's hands in her own. "Mrs. Wilcox—Laura Lee—has succumbed to her illness."

Dr. Ambrose wagged his head and ran a hand over his face. "She might have survived if she didn't have an underlying heart condition. I believe the severe bouts of coughing she's experienced recently weakened her heart to the point that it couldn't sustain her any longer." The two women forgotten, he moved away, murmuring to himself.

Chloe felt the cold creep into her very bones. She began to shutter and shake. Her mind struggled to comprehend what had happened. "But we were just talking a little bit ago. She told me how blessed she was." Chloe looked up at the nun in confusion.

"She was a wonderfully gracious lady. We'll all miss her."

Sister Rosemary joined them and wrapped a supportive arm around Chloe. "Let's get you back to your room, dear." At the end of the long hallway, the nun hugged her and turned her over to Prudence, who waited at the door to her room.

Somehow, she found herself tucked into bed. Sister Prudence poured a glass of water and sprinkled something in it. She pressed it to Chloe's lips.

"I don't want anything." She turned her face away.

"Dr. Ambrose prescribed a draught to help you rest. Please, Chloe, drink it."

Chloe's lips trembled. She looked back up at Prudence. "She knew she was dying, didn't she?"

The sister sat on the edge of the vacant bed. "Yes, she's known a long time. Really even before she came here. Laura Lee's family has been seeking a cure for her heart for years. They spent almost everything they had on doctors and experimental procedures. It became almost an obsession.

"When she contracted tuberculosis, she determined to find a place she could die in peace so they could live in peace." Prudence got up and came to lay a gentle hand along Chloe's cheek. "You made these last few days especially peaceful for her. Your love of life and sweet spirit were a balm to her soul."

Chloe was confused. "But she talked about how blessed she was. I don't understand."

"Laura Lee learned to see the blessings even in the midst of trials. Life is what we make of it. The good and bad are going to come. It's how we handle it that matters."

Chloe could see the wisdom in her words. Exhausted, she turned on her side and closed her eyes to say a prayer for her friend.

CHAPTER 41

By morning of the tenth day, Tyler was eager to return to Colorado Springs. Thoughts of seeing Chloe and playing catch with Hank filled his mind as he checked out of the National and headed to the depot. Victor was their first stop. Tyler got off to buy a newspaper to pass the time.

He was surprised to see Matthew Morrison leaning against a column, a canvas bag at his feet. The black man smiled when he turned and saw Tyler step down onto the platform.

"Thought you might be taking the same train." Matt pulled the piece of straw from his mouth. "John's stayin' behind to guard our claim and let his foot mend."

"Good idea, although your mother will be up in arms he didn't come along." Tyler pulled off his hat and ran a hand through his hair, then settled it back in place. "I wanted to get back early enough to see Chloe and Hank before I caught the afternoon train to Denver."

Matt's handsome face took on a serious expression. "Going to Denver to file your report?"

Tyler looked around to make sure they wouldn't be overheard. "There's a lot going on around here that bears watching. How much of it is being perpetrated outside the boundaries of the law is still yet to be determined."

Matt harrumphed. "Lawyer talk." He shook his head. "You gotta know there's some high rollers and low down scoundrels that are playin' fast and loose with the law. Money corrupts. It's a known fact. Why, I've seen even the most honest Joe trade in his morals for a chunk of gold. It does crazy things to people."

Tyler had to agree. That was why he needed to learn what James Archer's involvement was and where he stood. Something wasn't right, and he needed to know what was really going on. "I'll know more when I come back. What I do will depend on what I find out."

The train began to build up a head of steam and the conductor hung from the step to shout. "All abroad who's comin' abroad."

The rest of the train ride, Matt and Tyler got to know each other a bit better. Tyler liked what he saw in the man. Matthew Morrison was solid and dependable and knew what hard work and loyalty was all about. What he knew of John told him he was like his brother. Tyler hoped so, because he was likely going to need to count on them in the future in more ways than one.

By ten o'clock the two men stepped off the train and caught a trolley to Clare and Abel's. Tyler hung around long enough to find out Hank had spent the night with a friend and wouldn't be home until around lunchtime. It was good to know the lad had already made friends at school and was settling in. That left him the rest of the morning to see Chloe. The anticipation and anxiety had been building. Would she be better? It had been less than two weeks, but he hoped to see an improvement.

❧

Tyler stood in Glockner's main reception area, about to do battle with Sister Mary Margaret. Arms crossed and a firm line to her mouth, the nurse shook her head one more time. He took a deep breath in and let it out slowly to control his temper. "I understand you have rules, and I don't mean to disregard them, but I really need to see my wife. I'll take whatever precautions you feel are necessary."

"What seems to be the problem?"

Tyler recognized the doctor, who came to stand beside the nun. "Dr. Ambrose, pleasure to see you again. I was just requesting to see my wife, Chloe Reynolds."

"She's been here what—ten, eleven days now? That's hardly enough time to let her get settled. If you read through the information we gave you when you first arrived, you'll remember we strongly recommend non-fraternizing between guests and outsiders for the first month. It's for their own good, so they have time to build their systems back up."

Tyler didn't want to lose control in front of the sister or the doctor, but he wasn't about to concede to their rules. He huffed out his exasperation and tried to relax his clinched fists. Losing his temper wouldn't do anybody any good, least of all Chloe.

He put on his best lawyer face. "I assure you I read every sentence of your admission form and I remember it stating these were recommendations, not strict rules. Therefore, it should be at my own prerogative and discretion whether I abide by those recommendations. I know you have your patient's best interest at heart, but Chloe *is* my heart. Your job is to provide her with shelter, nutritious food, and round-the-clock care. Her family's job—my job—is to provide her with love and support. That's got to be worth something."

"He's right. The love and support of family is as important as anything we offer our guests." A young nun stepped up and extended her hand, her blue eyes warm and friendly. "I'm Sister Prudence, Chloe's main caregiver. Your wife is progressing wonderfully and may I say she is a delightful addition here at Glockner." She turned to the doctor and Sister Superior. "I'm taking Mr. Reynolds to see his wife now. I'm sure you'll be wanting to speak with me. I'll come to your office as soon as we're through." With a decisive tilt to her head, she smiled at Tyler. "I

The nun was every bit as feisty and strong willed as Chloe. Tyler imagined them getting along splendidly. "I hope I didn't get you into any trouble, Sister."

"Some things are worth fighting for. Like her." The sister pointed to the figure sitting emotionless in a nearby rocking chair. He stepped through the doorway leading out onto the wide veranda. Chloe sat cocooned in a quilt even though it was a warm spring day. Her beautiful black hair lay in long tresses over the patchwork and surrounded her delicate features. The dark splash of her lashes accentuated the paleness of her skin. *She looks so fragile.* As he drew closer, he could see a hint of rose to her cheeks and they seemed fuller to him. He didn't want to wake her, but his time was limited.

Sister Prudence put a hand on Tyler's arm. "Remember, you can't kiss. It would be too dangerous. If she starts to cough, you need to step away. The sputum is what holds the contagion. When you're done visiting, use the restroom and wash your hands thoroughly with hot, soapy water."

The nurse moved back inside.

Tyler was glad Chloe choose a sunny spot away from the others. He kneeled beside her and let his fingers dance along the smooth curve of her jaw. "Darling, wake up and let me see those beautiful brown eyes."

❧❦

Chloe stirred. She had been having the more wonderful dream. Her eyelids fluttered and widened in surprise. She smiled and pressed her face into Tyler's palm. "I dreamed you were here."

"You don't know how much I want to kiss you right now."

Alarmed, she pulled a hand out from under the cover. "You mustn't. It wouldn't be safe." She needed to feel his arms around her, to hear his heartbeat and smell the scent that was his alone. "Would you pick me up and hold me?"

Tyler gathered her in his strong, protective arms. She laid her head on his shoulder and breathed in the musky smell of him. He carried her down the steps and across the lawn to the edge of the flowerbeds. His eyes took in the grandeur before them. "I love these mountains." He gazed down at her. "But I love you more." His arms tightened around her.

This was where she belonged. This was home.

THE END

Dear Reader,

At the start of Fragile Reprieve, I had a completely different destination in mind. Now that I'm at the end, I see why Tyler and Chloe took me on this journey. I learned so much from them as they walked the cobbled streets of New York's slums and traveled to the mountains and mines of Colorado.

In this process, I discovered a wealth of information about our twenty-sixth president, Theodore Roosevelt, and what led up to his presidency. Life was not always kind to him, but the great losses he suffered shaped him into the man he would become. TR was a man of action, who lived life with vigor, and who cared deeply. I hope he would have been pleased with how I portrayed him.

In the world we live in today, we don't know what it was like for immigrant families where children as young as six and seven were forced to work ten to twelve-hour days in sweatshops, mills, mines, and factories. They struggled to survive in miserable conditions with inadequate food and shelter. The harsh reality is that many did not make it.

We are blessed to live in a time when science and modern medicine have virtually eradicated diseases like tuberculosis, Smallpox, and Diphtheria. The White Plague—tuberculosis—was no respecter of persons. It would come to take the young family living in the tenements and the famous like John Keats, Edgar Allan Poe, Eleanor Roosevelt, Babe Ruth, Paul Gauguin, and Nelson Mandela. Hundreds of thousands in America alone succumbed to the dreaded 'wasting disease'.

As the nineteenth century marched into the twentieth, one hope was found for the two to three million Americans diagnosed with TB—clean air and sunshine. Touted as a cure because of its high altitude, restorative air, and dry climate, thousands flocked to the foothills and mountains of Colorado. This rush of desperate cure-seekers changed the very makeup of this great state. Many of the hospitals we look to for medical care today started out as tuberculosis sanatoriums like Penrose Hospital in Colorado Springs, which was once the Glockner Sanatorium.

You may wonder how Chloe's journey will end and if Tyler will be able to right the wrongs he discovers in the mining district. I can't tell you because I don't know yet. We'll have to find out together in the next book 'Final Justice'

Thank you for turning the pages. I hope you came to care about the characters like I did. I have a feeling their story will go on.

Blessings,

Debra Shelton

July 2021 Update

As the 2nd edition of Fragile Reprieve goes to print, I am amazed at the parallels the world faces today as we continue to battle the deadly virus, COVID-19. We, as a modern world people, though we were beyond the ravaging capabilities of the microscopic world. Today, we know just how vulnerable we still are.

I pray God's protection surrounds you, and His blessings abound as we continue to walk through this fragile life.

Books by Debra Shelton

ESCAPING THE DARKNESS

Journey to Sanctuary
Journey to Freedom

WILD JUSTICE

Book 1: Second Chances
Book 2: Fragile Reprieve
Book 3: Final Justice

A ROCKY MOUNTAIN MEDLEY NOVELLA

Price of Grace